I0535267

# The Friends & Other Stories by Stacy Aumonier

Stacy Aumonier was born at Hampstead Road near Regent's Park, London on 31st March 1877.

He came from a family with a strong and sustained tradition in the visual arts; sculptors and painters.

On leaving school it seemed the family tradition would also be his career path. In particular his early talents were that of a landscape painter. He exhibited paintings at the Royal Academy in the early years of the twentieth century.

In 1907 he married the international concert pianist, Gertrude Peppercorn, at West Horsley in Surrey. A year later Aumonier began a career in a second branch of the arts at which he enjoyed a short but outstanding success—as a stage performer writing and performing his own sketches.

The Observer newspaper commented that "...the stage lost in him a real and rare genius, he could walk out alone before any audience, from the simplest to the most sophisticated, and make it laugh or cry at will."

In 1915, Aumonier published a short story 'The Friends' which was well received (and was subsequently voted one of the 15 best stories of 1915 by the Boston Magazine, Transcript).

Despite his age in 1917 at age 40 he was called up for service in World War I. He began as a private in the Army Pay Corps, and then transferred as a draughtsman in the Ministry of National Service.

By now he had four books published—two novels and two books of short stories—and his occupation is recorded with the Army Medical Board as 'author.'

In the mid-1920s, Aumonier received the shattering diagnosis that he had contracted tuberculosis. In the last few years of his life, he would spend long spells in various sanatoria, some better than others.

Shortly before his death, Stacy Aumonier sought treatment in Switzerland, but died of the disease in Clinique La Prairie at Clarens beside Lake Geneva on 21st December 1928. He was 55.

## Index of Contents

## The Friends

White and Mapleson often tried to recall the occasion when their friendship began, but neither succeeded. Perhaps it had its origin in some moment when the memory was to some extent blurred. Certain it is that they drifted together across the miasma of commercial London and founded a deep and lasting friendship that found its chief expression in the clinking of glasses in the saloon and luncheon bars of various hostelries off Oxford Street and Bloomsbury.

White acted as an agent for a firm of wire-mattress manufacturers in Old Street in the city, and as his business was conducted principally among the furnishing and upholstering businesses in the West End, and as Mapleson was the manager of the brass bed department at Tauntons, the large Furnishing Emporium in Bloomsbury, it is not surprising that they came in contact and that they had so many interests in common. There is, alas, no doubt that the most absorbing interest of both was the consumption of liquid refreshment, and there is also, alas, no doubt that the friendship was quickened by the curious coincidence of their mental vision when stimulated by alcoholic fumes. And it is here that one or two curious facts relating to the personalities of the two men should be noted. During the day, it would be no uncommon thing for either man to consume anything between ten and fifteen whiskies and sodas, and sometimes even more, yet of neither man could it be said I that he ever got really drunk. On the other hand, of neither man could it be said that he was ever really sober. White was of medium height, rather pale, and slight. He had a dark mustache and was always neatly dressed in a dark blue suit with well-fitting boots and gloves. He was extremely quiet and courteous in manner, and his manner varied but little. The effect of alcohol upon him was only to accentuate his courtesy and politeness. Toward the evening his lips would tremble a little, but he would become more and more ingratiating. His voice would descend to a refined gentle croon, his eyes would just glow with a sympathetic light, and he would listen with his head slightly on one side and an expression that conveyed the idea that the remarks of the speaker were a matter of great moment to him. Not that he did not speak himself; on the contrary, he spoke well, but always with a deferential timbre as though attuning himself to the mood and mental attitude of his companion.

On the other hand, Mapleson always started the day badly. He was a large, florid man with a puffy face and strangely colorless eyes. He wore a ponderous frock coat that was just a little out of date, with a waistcoat that hung in folds, and the folds never seemed free from sandwich crumbs and tobacco ash. He had an unfortunate habit with his clothes of never being quite quite inoffensive. That is to say, if he had on a new top hat his boots were invariably shabby, or if his boots were a recent acquisition his top hat would seem all brushed the wrong way. As I say, he always started the day badly. He would be very late and peevish and would fuss about with pills and cloves. He would complain of not being quite "thumbs up." Eleven fifteen would invariably find him round at "The Monitor," leaning against the mahogany bar and asking Mrs. Wylde to mix him "a whisky and peppermint" or some other decoction that between them they considered would be just the thing for his special complaint that morning." In the way of business," he would treat and be treated by several other pals in "the sticks," as this confraternity called the Furnishing Trade. It would be interesting to know what proportion of Mapleson's and White's income was devoted to this good cause. When Mapleson would arrive home, sometimes late at night, breathing heavily, and carrying with him the penetrating atmosphere of the taproom, he would say in response to the complaints of his tired wife, "I hate the stuff, my dear. You have to do it though. It's all in the way of business." A sociologist might have discovered (if he were searching for concrete instances) that White and Mapleson spent on each other every year very nearly eighty pounds, although the business they did together amounted to rather less than thirty, an unsound premium surely!

As the day wore on Mapleson would improve. And it was one of the assets of the White-Mapleson friendship that they usually did not meet till lunch-time. Then the two friends would clink glasses and stroll arm-in-arm into Polati's in Oxford Street, for, as Mapleson would say, "When a man works hard he needs feeding," and White would agree with him deferentially, and then they would secure a seat not too near the band, and, after thoroughly considering the menu, they would order a "mixed grill" as being "something English and that you can get your teeth into." During the interval of waiting for the mixed grill, which took fifteen minutes to prepare, Mapleson would insist on standing White a gin and bitters, and of course it was only right and courteous of White to return the compliment. The mixed grill would be washed down with a tankard of ale or more often with whisky and soda, after which the friends would sometimes share a Welsh rarebit or a savory; and it was Mapleson who introduced the plan of finishing the meal with a coffee and liqueur—"It stimulates one's mind for the afternoon's business," he would explain-and White flattered him on his good sense and insisted on standing an extra liqueur," Just to give value to one's cigar." Under the influence of these good things Mapleson would become garrulous, and White even more soothing and sympathetic. This luncheon interval invariably lasted two hours or two hours and a half. They would then part, each to his own business, while making an appointment to meet later in the afternoon at "The Duke of Gads-burg." And here a notable fact must be re- corded. For an hour or two in the afternoon each man did do some work. And it is a remarkable point that "Tauntons," the great house in Bloomsbury, always considered Mapleson a good salesman, as so indeed he was. The vast lapses of time that he spent away from business were explained away on the score of active canvassing. His turnover for the year compared favorably with that of the other managers at "Tauntons." While of White, strange rumors of the enormous fortune that he was accumulating were always current. The natural reserve of the wire-mattress agent, and his remarkable lucidity on matters of finance, added to the fact that he took in and studied "The Statist," gave him a unique position in the upholstering world. Men would whisper together over their glasses and say, "Ah, old White! he knows a thing or two!" and grave speculations would go on as to whether his income ran into four figures, and in what speculations he invested his money. Considerable profundity was given to these rumors by the fact that White always had money and that he was always willing to lend it. He carried a sovereign purse that seemed inexhaustible, Mapleson, on the other hand, though natively lavish, had periods of "financial depression." At these periods he would drink more and become maudlin and mawkish, and it was invariably White who helped him out of his troubles. The two friends would meet later in the afternoon "to take a cup of tea," and it often happened that Mapleson felt that tea would not be just the thing for his nervous constitution, so White would prescribe a whisky and soda, and they would adjourn to a place where such things may be procured. It is remarkable how quickly the time passed under these conditions, but just before six Mapleson would "run back to the shop to see if any orders had come in" With studious consideration, White would wait for him. It was generally half-past six or seven before Mapleson returned, thoroughly exhausted with his day's work.

It was then that the suavity and charm of White's manner was most ingratiating. He would insist on Mapleson having a comfortable seat by the fire in the saloon, and himself carrying across the drinks from the bar.

Mapleson soon became comforted and would suggest "a game of pills before going home." Nothing appealed to White more than this. For White was a very remarkable billiard player. Young Charlie Maybird, who is a furniture draughtsman and an expert on sport, used to say that White could give any pub. marker in London 40 in a 100 and beat him off the mark.

He had a curious, feline way of following the balls round the table; he seemed almost to purr over them, to nurse them and stroke them, and make them perform most astounding twists and turns. And each time he succeeded he would give a little sort of self-depreciatory croon, as much as to say, "I'm so sorry. I really don't know how the balls happen to do all this." And yet it is remarkable how often White lost, especially against Mapleson, Mapleson was one of those players who gave one the impression of being an expert on an off day. As a matter of fact, he never had an "on" day. He was just a very third-rate player, only he would attempt most difficult shots and then give vent to expressions of the utmost surprise and disgust that they didn't come off.

The billiards would last till eight o'clock or half past, when a feeling of physical exhaustion would prompt the arrangement that" a chop would be a good idea." They would then adjourn once more to the dining-room at "The Monitor" and regale themselves with chops, cheese, and ale, by which time Mapleson would arrive at the conclusion that it wasn't worth going home, so an adjournment would be made once more to the bar and the business of the evening would commence.

It might be worth while to recall one or two features of "The Monitor" bar, which was invariably crowded by salesmen and assistants from "Tauntons" and was looked upon as a sort of headquarters of the upholstering trade at that time. It was a large room, fitted in the usual way with glittering mahogany and small glass mirrors. Two long seats upholstered in green leather were set around a cheerful fireplace of blue tiles. There were also four small circular tables with marble tops, and on either side of the fireplace two enormous bright blue Daulton ware pots of hideous design containing palms. On the side facing the bar was a florid staircase with a brass handrail leading up to the dining and billiard-rooms.

The only difference that a stranger might have felt between this and any other place of a similar description at that time lay perhaps in its mental atmosphere. There was always a curious feeling of freemasonry. In addition to Mrs. Wylde there were two other barmaids, Nancie and Olive", who was also sometimes called "The Tit-mouse." They were both tall, rather thin girls, with a wealth of wonderful flaxen hair. They seemed to spend a considerable amount of time (when not engaged in serving) in brewing themselves cocoa and hot milk. Olive was a teetotaler and confessed frankly with regard to alcohol that she "hated the muck," but Nancie would occasionally drink stout.

To be served by Mrs. Wylde was a treat that only occasionally occurred to the more favored devotees of "The Monitor." She was a woman of enormous proportions with a white-powdered face, and also a wealth of flaxen hair. She invariably wore a rather shabby black dress trimmed with lace, and a huge bunch of fresh flowers, usually lilies and carnations.

Now everybody who came into the bar of "The Monitor" seemed not only to know Nancie and Olive and Mrs. Wylde by name, but everybody else by their name or nickname. For instance, this sort of thing would happen. A pale, thin, young man with pointed boots and a sort of semi-sporting suit would creep furtively in and go up to the bar and lean across and shake hands with Nancie and after a normal greeting would say, "Has the Captain been in?" and Nancie would reply, "Yes, he was in with the Babbit about four o'clock," and the young man would say, "Oh! didn't he leave nothing for me?" and Nancie would say, "No. I wouldn't be surprised if he came in later. 'Ere! I tell you what," and she would draw the young man to a corner of the bar and there would be a whispered conversation for a few moments, and then the young man would go out.

All of which would seem very mysterious to a casual visitor.

Of this atmosphere White and Mapleson were part and parcel. They had their own particular little round table near the fire, where, in spite of Mapleson's daily avowal to get home, one could rely on finding them nearly every evening. And they gathered around them quite a small colony of kindred spirits. Here they would sit very often till nearly twelve o 'clock when "The Monitor" shut, talking and drinking whisky. As the evening advanced Maple-son expanded. One of his favorite themes was Conscription. On this subject he and White were absolutely in accord. "Every man ought to be made to serve his country," Mapleson would say, bringing his fist down with a bang on the marble table. "He ought to be made to realize his civil responsibilities and what he owes to the Empire! Every man under thirty-five should serve three years" (Mapleson was forty-four). "It seems to me we're becoming a nation of knock-kneed, sentimental women."

And White would dilate upon what the Germans were doing and would give precise facts and figures of the strength of the German army, and the cost and probabilities of landing two army corps on the coast of Suffolk.

Another favorite theme was the action of "these silly women!" and Mapleson would set the bar in roars of laughter with a description of what he would do if he were Home Secretary.

Mapleson was very fond of talking about "his principles" In conversation it seemed that his actions must be hedged in by these iron-bound conventions. In effect they were practically as follows:

Business comes first, always.
Never fail to keep a business appointment.
Never mix port and whisky.
Never give anything to a stranger that you might give to a pal.

He had other rules of life, but they were concerned exclusively with rules of diet and drinking and need not concern us here.

Thoroughly exhausted with the day's business, Mapleson would leave the imperturbable White just before twelve o'clock, and not infrequently would find it necessary to take a cab to Baker Street to catch his last train to Willesden Green where he lived, and where he would arrive at night, having spent during the day a sum varying between twenty and thirty shillings, which was precisely the amount he allowed his wife every week to keep house for a family of five, and to include food, clothing, and washing.

White lived at Acton, and no one ever quite knew how he arrived there or by what means. But he never failed to report himself at nine o'clock the next morning at Old Street with all his notes, orders, and instructions neatly written out. It was remarkable how long "The Monitor" remained the headquarters of this fraternity, for, as one of them remarked, "the licensing business is very sensitive"; in the same way that a flock of crows will simultaneously and without any apparent reason fly from one hill to another, it will be a sort of fashion for a group of men to patronize a certain establishment and then suddenly to segregate elsewhere. It is true that there were one or two attempts at defection-Charlie Maybird once made an effort to establish a headquarters as far away as "The Trocadero" even, but the birds soon returned to the comforting hostelry of Mrs. Wylde.

And then one summer Mapleson was very ill. He got wet through walking to Baker Street one evening when, after having started, he found he had only three coppers on him. He traveled home in his wet clothes and next day developed a bad chill which turned into pneumonia. For days he lay in a critical state, but thanks to the attention of Mrs. Mapleson, who did not go to bed for three nights, and a careful doctor, he got over the crisis. But the doctor forbade him to go back to business for a fortnight and suggested that, if it were possible to arrange it, a few days at the seaside might set him up. White called several times, and was most anxious and solicitous, and assured Mrs. Mapleson that he would do anything in his power to help his friend, and sent a large basket of expensive fruits and some bottles of very old port wine.

Mapleson's illness, however, was of more troublesome a nature than appeared at first. After a rather serious relapse, the doctor said that his heart was not quite what it should be, and it was nearly a month before the question of moving him could be considered. Tauntons treated Mapleson very well over this, and his salary was paid every week, only of course he lost his commissions, which in the ordinary way represented the bulk of his income, and it became necessary for Mrs. Mapleson to economize with the utmost skill, especially as the invalid required plenty of good and well-cooked food on regaining his strength. The rest of the family had therefore to go on shorter commons than usual, and matters were not helped by the fact of one of the children developing glands and being in an enfeebled condition. White called one evening and was drinking a glass of the old port with the invalid, and they were discussing how it could be arranged for Mapleson to get a week at Brighton. "I think I could travel now," said Mapleson, "only I don't see how the Missus is going to leave Flora."

It was then that White had an inspiration. If it would help matters in the Mapleson family, he would be pleased to take a week off and go to Brighton with Mapleson. Mapleson hailed this idea with delight, and Mrs. Mapleson was informed on entering the room a little later, "You need not bother about it any more, my dear; White has been good enough to offer to go to Brighton with me." Mrs. Mapleson was a woman who said very little, and it was difficult on this occasion to know what she thought. In fact her taciturnity at times irritated Mapleson beyond endurance. She merely paused, drew in her thin, pale lips, and murmured, "All right, dear," and then busied herself with preparing Mapleson's evening broth.

The friends were very lucky with the weather. Fresh breezes off the Channel tempered the fierce August sun and made the conditions on the front delightful. It might be hinted that perhaps the weather might have been otherwise for the interest that they took in it.

For after the first day or so, finding his vitality returning to him, Mapleson soon persuaded his companion that the choicest spot in Brighton was the saloon bar of "The Old Ship." And he could not show his gratitude sufficiently. White was given carte blanche to order anything he liked.
But White would not listen to such generosity. He knew that the expenses that Mapleson had had to endure must be telling on him, so he insisted on paying at least twice out of three times.

Mapleson acknowledged that it was "a hell of a worry and responsibility having a family to keep. They simply eat up the money, my dear chap."

The week passed quickly enough and soon both were back at their occupations in town. The friendship pursued the even tenor of its way, and it was fifteen months before any incident came to disturb it ....

Then one day in October something happened to White. He fell down in the street and was taken to a hospital. It was rumored that he was dead. Consternation prevailed in the upholstering confraternity, and Mapleson made anxious enquiries at the hospital bureau.

It was difficult to gather precise details, but it was announced that White was very ill and that a very serious operation would have to be performed. Mapleson returned to the bar of "The Monitor," harboring a nameless dread. A strange feeling of physical sickness crept over him. He sat in the corner of the bar sipping his whisky, enveloped in a lugubrious gloom. He heard the young sparks enter and laugh and joke about White. It was a subject of constant and cynical mirth. "Hullo," they would say; "heard about old White? He's done in at last!" and then there would be whisperings and chucklings, and he would hear, "Drunk himself to death,"

"Doesn't stand a dog's chance, my dear chap; my uncle had the same thing. Why, he's been at it now for about twenty-five years-can't think how he's lasted so long!" And then they would come grinning up to Mapleson, hoping for more precise details. "Sorry to hear about your friend, Mr. Mapleson; how did it happen?..."

Mapleson could not stand it. He pushed back his half-filled glass and stumbled out of the bar. He was not conscious of an affection for White, or any sentiment other than a vast fear and a strange absorbing depression. He crept into the saloon of a small house off the Charing Cross Road, where no one would be likely to know him, and sat silently sipping from his glass. It seemed to have no effect upon him. The vision of White lying there-like Death- and perhaps even now the doctors were busy with their little steel knives ....

Mapleson shivered. He ordered more whisky and drank it neat. He stumbled on into other bars all the way to Trafalgar Square, drinking and wrestling with his fear. The spirits ultimately took their effect and he sat somewhere, in some dark corner, he could never remember where, with his mind in a state of trance. He remembered being turned out. It must have been twelve o 'clock-and engaging a cab- he could just remember his address-and ordering the man to drive home. In the cab he went sound asleep, hopelessly drunk, the first time for many years. He knew nothing more till the next day. Some one must have come down to help carry him in—he was no light weight-perhaps the cabman had to be bribed, too. He woke up about one o'clock feeling very ill and scared. He jumped up and called out, "What the devil's the time? What are we all doing? Why haven't I been called?"

Mrs. Mapleson came in-she put her hand on his forehead and said, "It's all right. I sent a telegram to say you were ill. You had better stop here. I'll get you some tea." Mapleson fell back on the pillows, and the sickening recollection of last night came back to him.

Later in the evening Mrs. Mapleson came in again and said, "I hear that Mr. White has had his operation and is going on as well as could be expected." Beads of perspiration streamed down Mapleson's face and he murmured, "My God! my God!" That was all that was said, and the next day Mapleson went back to work.

The officials at the hospital seemed curiously reticent about White. The only information to be gleaned for some days was that he was alive. Mapleson went about his work with nerveless indifference. He drank, but his drinking was more automatic than spontaneous. He drank from habit, but he gained neither pleasure nor profit from doing so.

The nameless fear pursued him. Great bags appeared under his eyes which were partly blood-shot. He stooped in his walk, and began to make mistakes in his accounts, and to be abstracted in dealing with customers.

He was arraigned before two of the directors of Tauntons, and one of them finished a harangue by suggesting that "it might be more conformable to business methods if he would remove the traces of yesterday's breakfast from the folds of his waistcoat." The large man received these criticisms in apathetic silence. "Poor old Mapleson!" they said round in the bar of "The Monitor."

"I've never seen a chap cut up so about anything as he is about White," and then abstract discussions on friendship would follow and remarkable instances of friendships formed in business.

Of course White would die-that was a settled and arranged thing, and curiously enough little sympathy was expressed, even by those to whom White had lent money.

In spite of his charm of manner and his generosity, they all felt that there was something about White they didn't understand. He was too clever, too secretive.

On Friday he was slightly better, but on Saturday he had a relapse, and on Sunday morning when Mapleson called at the hospital he was informed that White was sinking, and they didn't expect him to last forty-eight hours.

Mapleson had inured himself to this thought; he had made up his mind to this conclusion from the first, and this last intimation hardly affected him. He went about like one stunned, without volition, without interest. He was only conscious of a vast unhappiness and misery, of which White was in some way a factor.

For five days the wire mattress agent lay on the verge of death, and then he began to rally slightly. The house surgeon said it was one of the most remarkable constitutions he had ever come up against. For three days there was a distinct improvement, followed by another relapse. But still White fought on. At the end of another week he was out of danger. But the convalescence was long and tedious.

When at the end of six weeks he was well enough to leave the hospital, the house-surgeon took him on one side and said, "Now, look here, my friend; we're going to let you out. And there's no reason why you shouldn't get fairly well again. Only I want you quite to understand this: If you touch alcohol again in any form in any case for years-well, you might as well put a bullet through your own head." In another ten days White was back at business, looking exactly the same as ever, speaking in the same suave voice. He soon appeared in "The Monitor," but with the utmost courtesy declined all offers of drinks except ginger ale. It need hardly be said that to Mapleson such an event seemed a miracle. He had sunk into a low morbid condition from which he had never hoped to rise.

Out of courtesy the first evening Mapleson insisted on drinking ginger ale himself so that his friend should not feel out of it.

And they sat and had a long discussion into the night; White giving luminous and precise details of the whole of his illness and operation, eulogizing hospital methods and discussing the whole aspect of society toward therapeutics in a calmly detached way.

But Mapleson was not happy. He was glad to have White back, but the element of fear that White had introduced him to was not eliminated. He felt ill himself, and there somehow seemed a great gap between White in the old days and White drinking ginger ale and talking medicine! For three nights Mapleson kept this up and then thought he would have "just a nightcap. "

It gradually developed into the position that Mapleson resumed his whisky and White stuck to his ginger ale. And it is a curious fact that this arrangement depressed Mapleson more than it did White. He drank copiously and more frequently to try and create an atmosphere of his own, but always there was White looking just the same, talking just the same.

The ginger ale got on Mapleson's nerves. He felt that he couldn't stand it, and a strange and enervating depression began to creep over him again. For days this arrangement held good. White seeming utterly indifferent as to what he drank, and Mapleson getting more and more depressed because White didn't drink whisky. At length Mapleson suggested one evening that "surely just one" wouldn't hurt White. But White said with the deepest tone of regret that he was afraid it would be rather unwise, and, as a matter of fact, he had got so used to doing without it that he really hardly missed it.

From that moment a settled gloom and depression took hold of Mapleson. He just stood there looking at White and listening to him, but hardly troubling to speak himself. He felt utterly wretched. He got into such a state that White began to show a sympathetic alarm, and one evening toward the end of February as they were sitting at their favorite table in "The Monitor" White said, "Well, I'll just have a whisky and soda with you if you like."

That was one of the happiest evenings of Mapleson's life. Directly his friend began to drink some chord in his own nature responded, his eyes glowed, he became garrulous and entertaining.

They had another and then went to the Oxford Music Hall into the lounge, but there was such a crowd that they could not see the stage so they went to the bar at the back, and had another drink and a talk. How they talked that night! They talked about business, and about dogs, and conscription, and women, and the Empire, and tobacco, and the staff of Tauntons. They had a wild orgy of talk and drink. That night White drank eleven whiskies and sodas, and Mapleson got cheerfully and gloriously drunk.

It was perhaps as well that the friends enjoyed this bacchanale for it was the last time they met. By four o'clock the next afternoon White was dead ....

Mapleson heard of it the following night. He was leaning against the fireplace in" The Monitor," expatiating upon the wonderful improvement in White and extolling his virtues, when young Howard Aldridge, the junior salesman to Mr. Vincent Pelt, of Tauntons, came in to say that White's brother-in-law had just rung up Mr. Pelt to say that White was dead. When Maple-son heard this he muttered, "My Christ!"

These were the last words that Mapleson ever uttered in the bar of "The Monitor."

He picked up his hat and went out into the street. It was the same feeling of numbed terror and physical sickness that assailed him. With no plan of action arranged, he surprised his wife by arriving home before ten o'clock, and by going to bed. He was shivering. She took him up a hot-water bottle and she said, "I'm sorry to hear about White." Mapleson didn't answer, but his teeth chattered. He lay awake half the night thinking of Death ....

The next day he got up and went to business as usual. But for the second time the head of the firm felt it his duty to point out one or two cases of negligence to Mapleson and to warn him that "These things must not happen in the future."

Two days later Mapleson received a postcard signed by "F. Peabody" to say that the funeral of the late G. L. White would take place at such and such a church at East Acton and would leave the "Elms" Castlereach Road, Acton, at 12 o'clock, and it was intimated that a seat for Mr. Mapleson would be found in a carriage.

A fine driving rain out of a leaden sky greeted Mapleson when he. set out for White's funeral on the Saturday. His wife tried to persuade him not to go, for he was really ill. But he made no comment. He fiddled about with a Cassell's time table and could come to no satisfactory decision about the way to get there. His wife ultimately looked him up a train to Hammersmith from which terminus he could get a train. Before reaching Hammersmith a strange revulsion came over him. Why, after all, should he go to this funeral? White wouldn't know about it, and what did he know of White's relations! A strange choking and giddiness came over him, and at Hammersmith he found a comfortable refreshment room, where he partook himself, and decided that after refreshing he would go on to business.

After having two whiskies, however, he changed his mind. "No," he muttered to himself," I'll see it through." He boarded a tram that went in the direction of Acton. He found that he had to change trams at one point. It seemed an interminable journey. He kept wondering how White managed to get home at night from Oxford Street at 12 o'clock. He felt cold and wretched. The effect of the whisky wore off.

At last he reached Acton and asked for Castlereach Road. Nobody seemed to know it. He was directed first in one direction and then in another; at last a postman put him on the right track, but suggested that as it was some way he might get a 'bus to Gaddes Green and then it was only about fifteen minutes' walk.

Mapleson set off, keeping a sharp lookout for a place of refreshment, for the reactionary spirit was once more upon him. The 'bus put him down at a forlorn looking comer where there was only a sort of workman's alehouse. "I expect I'll pass one on the way," he thought, and taking his directions from the assistant of a greengrocer's shop he set out once more through the rain.

The farther he went the meaner and more sordid did the streets become. He did not pass a single public house that he felt he could approach. "I expect the neighborhood will change soon," he thought. "I expect I've come the wrong way. Why, every one said White must be making at least eight hundred a year! He wouldn't live in a place like this."

At length he came to a break in the neighborhood where some newly built villas crowded each other on the heels of the more ancient squalor. An errand boy told him that "Castlereach Road was the second turning on the right off Goldsmith's have-nue" He found Goldsmith's Avenue where a barrel organ was vomiting lugubrious music to an audience listening from the shelter of their windows, and swarms of dirty children were hurrying through the rain on nameless errands. A slice of bread and jam was thrown from a second story window to a little boy in the street and missed Mapleson's hat by inches. His progress was in any case the source of considerable mirth to the inhabitants.

At last he came to Castlereach Road. After the noise and bustle of Goldsmith's Avenue it seemed like the end of the world.

It was a long straight road of buff-colored villas with stucco facings and slate roofs, all identically the same. From the end where Mapleson entered it, it looked interminably and utterly deserted. Doubtless if it had been a fine day the gutters would have been crowded with children, but with the pouring rain there was not a soul in sight.

Mapleson blundered on in search of number 227, and as he did so a thought occurred to him that h6 and White had a common secret apart. He always had felt in his inmost heart a little ashamed of his red-brick villa in Willesden Green, and that was one reason why he had always kept business well apart from domestic affairs, and White had casually referred to "his place at Acton." His place at Acton! Mapleson entered it, horribly tired, horribly sober, horribly wretched. All the blinds were down. It had taken so long to get there he half hoped that he was too late.

A tall, gaunt woman in black with a slight down on her upper lip opened the door. She seemed surprised to see him.

He explained who he was.

She said, "Oh, yes. My! you are early. It's only half-past twelve!"

"Half-past twelve!" said Mapleson, "but I thought the funeral was to be at twelve."

Then the gaunt woman called into a little side room," 'Ere, Uncle Frank, what 'ave you been up to? Did you tell Mr. Maple that the funeral was at twelve?

"Oh, don't sye that! don't sye that!" came a voice from the room, and a small man with sandy hair and wizened features and small, dark, greedy eyes came out into the hall. "oh, don't sye that, Mr. Mapleson; I'm Peabody. I quite thought I said two o' clock!"

Mapleson had a wild impulse to whistle for a cab or a fire-engine and to drive away from this, anywhere. But the utter helplessness of his position held him fast. Before he had time to give the matter serious thought he was being shown into the drawing-room, a small stuffy room with a blue floral wall paper and bamboo furniture, and many framed photographs, and the gaunt woman was saying, "oh, Uncle Frank, how could you have made that mis-tyke!" And Uncle Frank was explaining how it might have occurred and at the same time saying that they must make the best of it, that Mr. Mapleson would have a bit of lunch, "there was a nice cut of cold leg of mutton and of course no one under circumstances like this would expect an elaborate meal; in fact no one would feel like it apart from anything else." And then the gaunt woman left the room, and Mapleson was alone with Uncle Frank.

Mapleson could not recollect ever having met any one whom he so cordially hated at sight. He had a sort of smug perpetual grin, a habit of running his hands down his thighs as far as his knees, and giving vent to a curious clicking noise with his cheeks. "Well, this is a very sad hocca-sion, Mr. Mapleson" he said; "very sad indeed. Poor George, did you know him well? Eva, his wife, you know, she's upstairs quite prostrate; that was her sister who showed you in. Yes, yes, well, how true it is that in the Midst of Life we are in Death! I 'm afraid poor George was careless, you know. Very careless! Clever, mind you, clever as they make 'em, but careless. Do you know, Mr. Maple-son, he hadn't even insured his life! And he's left no will! There isn't enough to pay his funeral expenses! Fortunately Eva's clever, oh, yes, she's clever with her fingers; they say there's no one in the neighborhood can touch her in the millinery. Oh, yes, she's been at it some time! Why, bless my soul, do you know she's paid the rent of this 'ouse for the last four years. Oh, she's a clever woman I Poor soul though, her great consolation is that George didn't die in the 'orspital. Yes, Mr. Mapleson, he died upstairs quiet as a lamb. She was there at the end-it was a great consolation!"

And Uncle Frank nodded his head and his little eyes sparkled, but the grin never left his lips. Mapleson said nothing, but the two men sat there in a somber silence, Uncle Frank occasionally nodding his head and muttering, "it's a sad hocca-sion!"

The rain increased and it seemed unnaturally dark in the blue drawing-room, and Mapleson felt that he had sat there an eternity, consumed by desire to get away, when there was another knock at the door, and a youth was let in.

Uncle Frank called him "Chris," and he seemed to be a cousin or some near relation of White's. He was a raw youth who had just gone to business and was very-conscious of his collars and cuffs. He seemed to take to Mapleson and he sat watching him furtively. Mapleson seemed so very much man of the world, so very desirable a personality. He made many advances to draw the large man out, but the latter felt a repugnance for him in only a slight less degree than in the case of Uncle Frank.

At length the gaunt sister asked them all into the dining-room, which was a room on the other side of the passage that seemed even smaller and stuffier than the drawing-room. It was papered with a dark red paper and the woodwork painted chocolate. As they crossed the hall they passed Mrs. White, who had apparently been persuaded by her sister "to try and take something."

She was a little shriveled person with white cheeks and her eyes were red with weeping.

She hurried by the men without speaking, and a curious thought struck Mapleson. During the twenty years or so that he had known White, he could not recollect him speaking of his wife. He probably had done so, but he could not recollect it. He remembered him talking about "his place at Acton" but never of his wife. He did not feel entirely surprised. White was probably ashamed.

In the window of the dining-room were several bird-cages containing two canaries, a bull-finch, and a small, highly colored bird, that hopped from the floor of its cage on to a perch and kept up a toneless squeak, with monotonous regularity. Uncle Frank went up to the cage and tapped the wires and called out, "Ah, there he is! cheep! cheep! This is our little Orstrylian bird.

Mr. Mapleson! Isn't he! Yes, yes, he's our clever little Orstrylian bird!" and during the course of the hurried meal of cold mutton and cheese, the birds formed a constant diversion. Uncle Frank would continually jump up and call out, "Oh, yes, he's our little Orstrylian bird!"

Mapleson tried to recall whether he had ever discussed birds with White, and he felt convinced that he had not. And yet it seemed a strange thing. White apparently had had these birds for some time, three different varieties in his own house! Mapleson would have enjoyed talking about birds with White; he could almost hear White's voice, and his precise and suave manner of discussing their ways and peculiarities. And the terrible thought came to him that he would never hear White talk about birds, never, never.

This breach of confidence on White's part of never telling him that he kept birds upset Mapleson even more than his breach of confidence in not talking about his wife.

"Oh, yes, he's a clever little Orstrylian bird!" A terrible desire came to Maple - son to throw Uncle Frank through the window the next time he heard this remark.

Before they had finished the meal three other male relations appeared, and a craving came over Mapleson for a drink. Then the sister came down with a decanter of sherry and said that perhaps the gentlemen would like some. Uncle Frank poured out a glass all round. It was thin sickly stuff and to the brass bed manager like a thimbleful of dew in a parched desert. A horrible feeling of repugnance came over him; of repugnance against all these people, against the discomfort he found himself in.

After all, who was White? When all was said and done White was really nothing to him, only a man he'd met in the course of business and had a lot of drinks and talked with. At that moment he felt he disliked White and all his sniveling relations.

He wanted to go, to get away from it all, but he couldn't see how. There was half a glass of sherry left in the decanter. He unblushingly took it as the funeral cortege arrived. There were two ramshackle carriages and a hearse and a crowd of dirty children had collected. He tried to mumble some excuse for not going, to Uncle Frank, but his words were lost by an intensely painful scene that took place in the hall as the coffin was being brought down. He did not notice that the sister with the down on her upper lip became an inspired creature for a few moments, and her face became almost beautiful....

He felt that he was an alien element among all these people, that they were nothing to him, and that he was nothing to them, and he felt an intense, insatiable desire for a drink. If he couldn't get a drink he felt he would go mad.

Some one touched him on the arm and said, "Will you come with us in the second carriage, Mr. Mapleson." He felt himself walking out of the house and through a row of dirty children. For a moment he contemplated bolting up the street and out of sight, but the feeling that the children would probably follow him and jeer paralyzed this action, and then he was in the carriage, with Chris and another male relation who was patently moved by the solemnity of the occasion.

Chris wriggled about and tried to engage him in banal conversation with an air that suggested, "Of course, Mr. Mapleson, this is a sad affair, but we men of the world know how to behave."

The dismal cortege proceeded at an ambling trot, occasionally stopping. Chris gave tip for the moment trying to be entertaining, and the forlorn relation talked about funeral services and the comfort of sympathy in time of bereavement. They crawled past rows of congested villas and miles of indescribable domesticity of every kind, till as they were turning round a rather broader avenue than usual where there were shops, the forlorn relation said, "We shall be in the cemetery in five minutes."

And then Mapleson had an inspiration. They were ambling along this dreary thoroughfare, when his eye suddenly caught a large and resplendent public house. It was picked out in two shades of green and displayed a gilt signboard denoting, "The Men of Kent."

Almost without thinking and certainly in less time than it takes to chronicle. Maple-son muttered something to his two companions and called out of the window to the driver to stop. He jumped out and called out to the driver of the hearse and the other carriage to stop, and then, before any one realized what it was all about, he darted into the saloon bar of "The Men of Kent."

The bar was fortunately empty, but through the little glass shutters two women and a man in the private bar watched the performance.

There was a moment of dazed surprise followed by a high shriek of laughter and a woman's voice in strident crescendo, "Oh, Gawd! He's stopped the funeral to come in an 'ave a drink! Oh, my Gawd!" Mapleson's tongue seemed to cling to the roof of his mouth but he gasped out an order for a whisky and soda. To the barman these incidents were nothing and he served the drink instantly, but to the three in the private bar it was a matter of intense enjoyment. The other woman took it up. "Well, I'm damned! That's the first time! We known that 'appen—Gawd I fancy stoppin' a funeral to come and 'ave a drink!" and then the other woman,

"Lap it up, Charlie! won't you let me 'ave a drop, old bird!" and the man bawled out," 'Ere, I sye, ain't the others comin' in! Let's make a dye of it!"

The women continued shrieking with laughter, and the appalling ignominy of his position came home to him. He knew that he was damned in the eyes of White's friends.

Curiously enough the thought of White had passed out of his mind altogether. He was a thing in revolt against Society, without feelings, and without principles.

Yet when the whisky was put in front of him, his hand trembled and he could not drink it. He fumbled with the glass, threw down sixpence and darted out of the bar again.

In the meanwhile, Uncle Frank and other members of the funeral party had got out of the carriages and were having a whispered consultation on the curb. Instructions had evidently been given for the cortege to proceed, for Uncle Frank was talking to the driver of the hearse when Maple-son appeared.

As they all got back into the carriages, the three people came out of the bar and raised a cheer, and one of the women called out, "Oh, don't go, dearie! come back and fondle me!" and the other two started a song and dance on the pavement. Maple-son lay all of a heap in the corner of the carriage and he noticed that he was alone with Chris. The forlorn relation had gone into the other carriage.

In a few minutes they arrived at a church, a large new building with early Victorian Gothic arches and a profusion of colored glass. The funeral party huddled together in the gloom of the large church, and some- how the paucity of their numbers seemed even more depressing than the. wretchedness of their appearance.

Mapleson sat a little way back, and curiously enough his mind kept reverting during the service to the little birds. He felt a distinct grievance against White on account of the little birds. Why hadn't White told him? especially about the small Australian bird? It would have made a distinctly interesting subject of conversation.

The service seemed interminably long, and it was a relief when the tall, rather good-looking young clergyman led the way out into the cemetery. The rain was still driving in penetrating gusts, and as they stood by the graveside the relations looked askance at each other, uncertain whether it was the proper thing to do to hold up an umbrella. As to Mapleson, he was indifferent. For one thing he had not brought an umbrella. But it seemed frightfully cold.

They lowered the coffin into the grave and earth was sprinkled. For. a second it flashed through his mind, "That's White being let down," and then a feeling of indifference and repugnance followed, and the craving desire to get away from all these sordid happenings. Then he suddenly thought of White's wife. "A miserable looking slattern, she was!" he thought. "Why, what was she sniveling about! What could she have been to White, or White to her? Why, he never mentioned her during twenty years!"

He experienced a slight feeling of relief when the service finished and the party broke up, and he hastily made for the cemetery gates, knowing that White's friends would be as anxious to avoid him as he was to avoid them, but he had not reached them before some one came hurrying behind and caught him up.

It was the young man named Chris. "I expect you're going up west, Mr. Maple-son," he said. "If it's not putting myself in the way, I'll come too." Mapleson gave an inarticulate grunt that conveyed nothing at all, but the young man was not to be put off.

There was something about the bulk of Mapleson and the pendulous lines of his clothes and person that made Chris feel when he was walking with him that he was "knocking about town" and "mixing with the world." He was himself apprenticed to a firm of wall-paper manufacturers, and he felt that Mapleson would be able to enlighten him on the prospects and the outlook of the furnishing and decorating trade. He talked gaily of antique furniture till they came to a gaunt yellow brick station.

On enquiry there seemed to be no trains that went from it to any recognizable or habitable spot, but outside were two melancholy hackney carriages. By this time Mapleson was desperate and a strange feeling of giddiness possessed him.

He got in and told the driver vaguely "to drive up to London." Chris came to the rescue and explained to him that he might drive to Shepherd's Bush first. They started off and rattled once more through the wilderness of dreary villas.

The young man accepted the position he found himself in with perfect composure. He attributed Mapleson's silence to an expansive boredom, and he talked with discretion and with a sort of callous tact. Before they reached Shepherd's Bush, however, Mapleson muttered something about feeling faint, and Chris immediately suggested that they should go and have a drink. "You might bring me something in" said Mapleson. "I'll have a brandy-neat. "They drove helplessly through neat avenues and roads for nearly ten minutes without passing anything in the way of a public house. At last they came to a grocer's shop, licensed to sell spirits not to be consumed on the premises. "Go and buy me a bottle of brandy" said Mapleson, The young man got out and soon returned with a six-and-sixpenny bottle of Hennessy's three star brandy and a corkscrew. He paid for it himself, relying on the natural honor of Mapleson to settle up afterwards, but the matter was never mentioned again.

He drew the cork, and Mapleson took a long swig and then wiped the mouth of the bottle and offered it to Chris. Chris behaved like a man and also took a draft but spluttered rather.

For the rest of the journey Mapleson at regular intervals took thoughtful and meditative swigs and gradually began to revive. He went so far as to ask Chris if he knew anything about the little birds and how long White had had them. Chris said he knew he had had the canaries for four or five years and the bullfinch for two years. He didn't know much about the little Australian bird. This information seemed to cause Mapleson to revert to his former gloom.

When they reached Shepherd's Bush the cabman refused to go farther. So they got out and got into another cab, Mapleson carrying the brandy bottle under his arm. He took it upon himself to tell the cabman-this time a taxi- ' to drive round the Outer Circle of Hyde Park and to take the damned hood down."

It was about half-past four when they reached Hyde Park and the rain had ceased a little. It was the fashionable hour for the afternoon drive. Magnificent motors and two-horse phaetons were ambling round well within the regulation limit. Their cab was soon almost hemmed in by the equipages of the great world. But after they had completed the circle once, and Mapleson lay back with his feet on the opposite seat, and his hat all brushed the wrong way, and without the slightest compunction held the large brandy bottle to his lips every few yards, Chris began to feel that there was a limit to his desire to "mix with the world."

He got the cab to stop near the Marble Arch, and explained to Mapleson that he must get out and take the tube to business.

And then there was a scene. Mapleson, who up to that time had not addressed a personal word to Chris, suddenly became maudlin. He cried, and said that he had never taken to any one as he had to Chris; he was the dearest fellow in the world; he mustn't leave him; now that White was dead he was the only friend he had.

But people began to collect on the sidewalk and Chris simply ran off. The taxi- driver began to be suspicious about his fare which was registered fourteen shillings. But Mapleson gave him a sovereign on account and told him to drive to Cleopatra's Needle on the Embankment.

By the time they reached there the brandy bottle was three quarters empty and tears were streaming down his cheeks. He offered the driver a drink, but the driver was not "one of that sort" and gruffly suggested that Mapleson "had better drive 'ome." So he got out of the cab pathetically and settled with the driver and sat on a seat of the Embankment, hugging his bottle and staring at the river.

Now it is very difficult to know exactly what Mapleson did the rest of that afternoon between the time when he dismissed the cabman and half-past eight when he turned up in the bar of "The Monitor."

It is only known that he struggled in there at that time, looking as white as a sheet. He was wet through, and his clothes were covered with mud. He struggled across to the comer where he and White used to sit, and sat down. The bar was fairly crowded at the time, and young Chris made his debut there. He felt that he would be a person of interest. When Mapleson appeared he went up to him, but Mapleson didn't know him, and said nothing.

Several others came up and advised Mapleson to go home and change his clothes and have a drink first, but he just stared stupidly ahead and made no comment. Some one brought some whisky and put it before him, but he ignored it. They .then came to the conclusion that he was ill, so they sent for a cab and two of them volunteered to see him home.

Just as they were about to lead him out, he stood up. He then stretched out his arms and waved them away. He picked up the glass of whisky and raised it slowly to his lips. But before it reached them he dropped it and fell backwards across the table.

"Women, you know," said Charlie May-bird the other day, addressing two friends in "The Monitor" "—are silly creatures. They think love and friendship is all a question of kissin' and cuddlin' They think business is all buyin' and sellin'; they don't think men can make friendships in business. Crikey! I reckon there's more friendships made in business-real friendships, I mean-than ever there is outside. Look at the case of White and Mapleson! I tell you those two men loved each other! For over twenty years they were inseparable; there was nothing they would not have done for each other; hand and glove they was over everything. I've never seen a chap crumple up so as Mapleson did when White died; in fact, from the very day when White was took ill. He went about like a wraithe. I'll never forget that night when he came in here after the funeral. He sat over there, look, by the fireplace. He looked as though his 'eart was broken I Suddenly he stood up and lifted his glass and then dropped it and then fell backwards crash on to the floor! They carried him and took him to the 'orspital, but he never regained consciousness. The doctors said it was fatty degeneration of the 'eart, 'elped on by some kidney trouble. But I know better! He died of a broken 'eart. Lord, yes; I tell you there's a lot of romance in the furnishing trade!"

"Did he leave any money?" asked one of the friends.

"My word, yes! More than White," answered the genial Charles. "White never left a bean, and it seems his missus had not only been paying the rent out of her millinery but allowed White some. White was a card, he was!"

"And what did Mapleson leave!"

"Mapleson left nearly four pounds!"

"'S truth! is that all?"

"Four pounds and a wife and five kids, the eldest twelve!"

"A wife and five kids! How the hell does she manage to keep things going?"

"Oh. Gawd knows! Come on, let's go over to the Oxford and see what's on!"


## The Packet

Mr. Bultishaw stood leaning heavily against the bar in 'The Duchess of Teck," talking to his friend, Mr. Ticknett. Their friendship had endured for nearly twenty-seven years, and they still called each other "Mr." Bultishaw and "Mr" Ticknett. They were on the surface a curiously ill-matched couple, and the other salesmen and buyers from Cotterway's could never see what they had in common. Bultishaw was a big puffy man, shabbily florid. He had a fat babyish face, with large bright eyes which always seemed to be on the verge of tears, but whether this condition of liquefaction was due to his excessive emotionalism, or to the generally liquid state of his whole body, it would be difficult to decide. He was of an excitable nature, and though his voice seemed to come wheezing through various local derangements of his system, and was always pitched in a low key, it suggested a degree of excitement-usually of a querulous kind-quite remarkable in a person of his appearance. He was a man of moods, too. He was not always querulous, in fact his querulousness might generally be traced to an occasional revolt of his organic system against the treatment to which it was normally subjected. There were times when he was genial, playful, kind, sentimental, and maudlin. His clothes had a certain pretentiousness of style and wealth, not sustained by the dilapidated condition of their linings and edges, and the many stains of alcohol and the bums from matches and tobacco carelessly dropped. He was the manager of the linoleum department at Cotterway's.

Ticknett had a similar position with regard to "soft goods" in the same firm. But in appearance and character he was entirely dissimilar to Bultishaw. One of the junior salesmen one day called him "The Chinese God," and there was indeed something a little Eastern in his reserved manner, his suavity, and his great capacity for apparently minding his own business and yet at the same time-well, nobody liked Ticknett, but they all admired his ability, and most of them feared him. He was admired because he had risen from the position of being a "packer" in the yard to that of great influence, and he even shared the confidence of Mr. Joseph Cotterway himself. His skin was rather yellow, and he had very heavy black eyebrows and mustache and deep-set eyes with a slight cast. His clothes were so well cut that in the bar of "The Duchess of Teck" they seemed almost assertively unobtrusive.

Bultishaw was a prolific talker, and Ticknett was a patient listener. This was perhaps one of their principal bonds of mutual understanding. They had, of course, one common interest of an absorbing nature. It bubbled and sparkled in the innumerable glasses which, at all hours of the day, Mrs. Clarke and Daphne and Gladys handed to them across the bar of "The Duchess of Teck," which in those days was always crowded with the salesmen and the staff of Cotterway's.

On this particular morning, Bultishaw was holding a glass in his fat fingers, and breathing heavily between each sentence. He was saying:

"'Sperience is the thing that counts in the furnishing trade, like anywhere else- ugh! Take any line you like-ugh!—buying cork carpets, eating oysters, or extending the Empire-ugh!—it's the man with 'sperience who counts. These young fellers! ... ugh! ... "

Bultishaw shrugged his shoulders expressively, and glanced round the bar. Immediately a change came over his expression. His eyes sparkled angrily, and he shook the dregs of whisky in his glass, and drank them off with a spluttering gulp. Ticknett followed the glance of his friend and was quickly observant of the reason of Bultishaw's sudden trepidation. "Percy" had entered the bar. Percy was Bultishaw's assistant and also his bete-noir.

He was a slim young man dressed in a most extravagant manner. He had a pale face, and a slightly receding chin. He wore a small bowler hat with a very narrow brim, pointed patent leather boots, a very shapely overcoat which almost suggested that he wore corsets, a pale lemon tie held together by a gold pin, and a spotted green waistcoat.

Percy was a very high-spirited young person-an irrepressible-with a genius for taking stage center. He was invariably accompanied by several friends of his own age, and he had a habit of greeting a whole barful of men, whether he knew them or not, with a cheering cry of:

"Hullo! hullo! HULLO! So here we all are!"

He would deliver this greeting with such a gay abandon that every one would look up and laugh. Men would nod, and call out:

"Hullo! here's Percy! How do, Percy?"

And even those who did not know him would be conscious of some contagious fever of geniality. The conversation would grow louder and livelier, and Percy would invariably become the center of a laughing group.

In spite of his extravagance of manner, his irresponsibility, his passion for misquoting poetry, he had been marked down by several discriminating heads of the firm as" a smart boy."

He was indeed a very smart boy, from his gay clothes to his sparkling repartee with Daphne and Gladys. To Daphne it was known that he was an especial favorite. He would hold her hand across the bar, and smile at her engagingly, and say:

"And how is the moon of my delight?" And other enigmatic and brilliant things.

And Daphne would look at him with her sleepy, passionate eyes, and say: "Oh, go on! You are a one!"

She was a silent little thing, incredibly ignorant. She was not pretty, but she had masses of gold-brown hair, and a figure rather over-developed. There was about her something extremely attractive to the men who frequented "The Duchess of Teck," a kind of brooding motherliness. She had an appealing way of sighing, and her eyes were always watchful, as though in the face of every stranger she might discover the solution of her troubles.

Bultishaw hated Percy for several reasons. One was essentially a question of personality. He hated his aggressive exuberance, his youthfulness, his ridiculous clothes, his way of brushing back his hair, and incidentally of scoring off Bultishaw. He hated him because he had the habit of upsetting the placid calm of "The Duchess of Teck." He created a restlessness. People did not listen so well when Percy was in the room.

Moreover, he hated the way he took possession of Daphne. It is difficult to know what Bultishaw's ideas were with regard to Daphne. He was himself a widower, aged fifty-six, and he lived in a small flat in Bloomsbury with his two daughters, who were both about Daphne's age. He never made love to her, but he treated her with a sort of proprietary sense of confidence. He told her all about himself. In the morning when the bar was empty he would expatiate on the various ailments which had assailed him overnight, his sleeplessness, his indigestion, his loss of appetite. And he found her very sympathetic. She would say:

"Oh, reely, Mr. Bultishaw! I am sorry! It's too bad! Have you ever tried Ponk's Pills!"

They would discuss Ponk's Pills exhaustively, and their effect on the system, but eventually Mr. Bultishaw would say that he thought he would try "just a wee drop of Scotch." And so he would start his day.

It must, alas I be acknowledged that the accumulated years of his convivial mode of life were beginning to tell on Bultishaw.

He was not the man he was. At his best he was a good salesman. He knew the cork lino industry inside out. He had had endless experience. But there were days of fuddlement, days when he would make grievous mistakes, forget appointments, go wrong in his calculations. And the directors were not unobservant of the deterioration of his work and of his personal appearance. There was a very big rumor that Bultishaw was to be superseded by a younger man. This rumor had reached Bultishaw himself, and he accepted it with ironic incredulity.

"How can any one manage lino without 'sperience?" he said.

Nevertheless the rumor had worried him of late, and had increased his sleeplessness. He was conscious of himself-the vast moral bulk of himself rolling down the hill. He knew he would never be able to give up drinking. He had no intention of trying. He had been at it too long. He had managed in his time to save nearly a thousand pounds. If he were sacked it would bring in a little bit, but not enough to live on. About fifty pounds a year, but he spent quite this amount in the bar of "The Duchess of Teck" alone. He would have to hunt round for another job. It would be ignominious, and it might be difficult to secure at his age.

This was, then, another reason for disliking Percy, for "The smart boy's" name had been mentioned in this very connection. And what did this soapy headed young fool know about cork carpets!

What 'sperience had he had! A paltry two years. He was, too, so insufferably familiar and insolent. He had even once had the audacity to address Bultishaw as "Mr. Bulky-chops," a pseudonym that was not only greeted with roars of laughter but had been adopted by others.

On this morning then when Percy made his accustomed entrance with its bravura accompaniment: "Hullo! Hullo! HULLO! So here we all are!"

Mr. Bulti-shaw's hand trembled, and he turned his back and muttered: "That young—!" The yellow face of Ticknett turned in the direction of Percy, but it was quite expressionless and he made no comment. He lighted another cigarette and looked across the bar at Daphne. The girl's cheeks were dimpled with smiles. Percy was talking to her. Suddenly Ticknett said to her in his chilling voice:

"I want two more Scotch whiskies and a split soda."

The girl looked up, and the dimples left her cheeks. She seemed almost imperceptibly to shrink within herself. She poured out the drinks and handed them to Ticknett. Bultishaw continued his querulous complaints about the insolence of young and ignorant men, trying to oust older and more- experienced men from their hardly fought for positions.

And Ticknett listened, and his dark mustache moved in a peculiar way as he said:

"Yes, yes, I quite agree with you, Mr. Bultishaw. It's too bad."

A week later there was a sudden and dramatic turn of events in the firm of Cotterway's. Much to everybody's surprise, Percy was suddenly sacked without any reason being given, and Bultishaw was retained. In fact, Bultishaw was given another two years' contract on the same terms as before. To what extent Ticknett was responsible for this development or what was really at the back of it all, nobody was ever quite clear. It is certain that on the day of Percy's dismissal these two friends dined together, and spent an evening of a somewhat bacchanalian character. It is known that at that time Ticknett had been conspicuously successful over some deal in tapestries with a French firm, and that he had lunched one day alone with Mr. Joseph Cotterway. It is doubtful even whether he ever gave the precise details of his machinations to Bultishaw himself. The result certainly had the appearance of quickening their friendship. They called each other "dear old feller," and there were many whispered implications about "insolent young swine."

The career of Percy was watched with interest. Of course he took his dismissal with a laugh, and entertained a party of his friends to a hilarious farewell supper.

But it happened that that summer was a peculiarly stagnant one in the furnishing world. The brilliant youth did not find it so easy to secure another situation. He was observed at first swinging about the West End in his splendidly nonchalant manner, and he still frequented the bar of "The Duchess of Teck". But gradually these appearances became more rare. As the months went by he-began to lose a little of his self-assurance and swagger, and it is even to be regretted that his gay clothes began to show evidences of wear. He once secured a situation at a small firm in Bays-water, but at the end of three weeks he was again dismissed, the proprietor going bankrupt owing to some unfortunate speculation. It would be idle to imagine what Percy's career would have been had not the war broken out in August when he was still out of employment. He volunteered for service the morning after war was declared, and then indeed there was a great scene of bibulous enthusiasm in "The Duchess of Teck" He was toasted and treated, and every one was crying out:

"Well, good luck, Percy, old man."

And Percy was in the highest spirits, and borrowed money from every one to stand treat to every one else. And Daphne cried quite openly, and in the corner of the bar Bultishaw was whispering to Ticknett:

"This'll knock the starch out of the young swine" And Ticknett replied:

"He'll get killed."

There was at times a certain curious finality about Ticknett's statements that had a way of making people shudder.

Bultishaw laughed uncomfortably and repeated: "It'll knock the starch out of him."

The departure of Percy was soon almost forgotten in the bewilderment of drama that began to convulse Europe. Others went also. There was upheaval, and something of a panic in the furnishing world. Every man had his own interests to consider, and there was the big story unfolding day by day to absorb all spare attention. Perhaps the only man among all the devotees of "The Duchess of Teck" who thought considerably about Percy was Bultishaw. It was very annoying, but he could not dismiss the young man from his thoughts.

When the autumn came on, and the cold November rains washed the London streets, Bultishaw would suddenly think of Percy and he would shiver. Percy had been sent to some camp in Essex for his training, and often in the night Bultishaw would wake up and visualize Percy sleeping out in the open, getting wet through to the skin, possibly getting rheumatic fever. He was a ridiculously delicate-looking young man, quite unfitted to be a soldier. It occurred to Bultishaw more than once that if he and Ticknett hadn't … if Percy had secured his position, which everybody said was his due … he wouldn't have been sent out into all this.

And "all this" was a terrible thing to Bultishaw. During the fifty-six years of his life he had made a god of comfort. He loved warmth, good cheer, food, drink, security. The alternative seemed to him hell. He could not believe that there could be any sort of compensation in discomfort, and hardship, in restraint, and discipline, and self-abnegation. It was the thing he could not understand. And then at the end was the Awful Thing itself. He could not bear to dwell on that. He drank more prodigiously than ever.

The firm of Cotterway's was reorganized, and Bultishaw would undoubtedly have had the sack if it had not been for his two years' contract. As it was, expenses in every respect were cut down, and Bultishaw's royalties only amounted to a very small sum. He lived above his salary, and broke into his capital. He seemed more and more to rely on Ticknett. The manager of soft goods seemed to him the one stable thing in a shifting world.

When Percy one day made his sudden, meteoric, and final appearance in "The Duchess of Teck" the whole thing seemed like a dream. The usual crowd was gathered just before lunch, drinking gins and bitters, and whisky, and beer, and talking about "our" navy, and "our" army, and "our" Government, and what "we" should do to the Germans, when the level hum of conversation was broken by a loud and breezy:

"Hullo! Hullo! HULLO! So here we all are!"

And lo! and behold, there was Percy, looking somehow bigger than usual, the general gaiety of his appearance emphasized by a pink complexion, a distinct increase of girthy and a beautiful khaki suit. And Bultishaw found himself clapped on the back and the same voice was exclaiming:

"Well, 'ow are you, Bulky-chops! Lookin' better than ever, 'pon my word!" And then the bar was immediately in a roar of conviviality. Everybody struggled for the honor of standing Percy drinks, for he explained that he was off the next day to France. It is to be feared that during that afternoon Percy got rather drunk. He certainly indulged in violent moods between boisterous hilarity and a certain sullen pugnacity. At intervals he would continually ask for Ticknett, but to Bultishaw's surprise, Ticknett had disappeared almost immediately Percy entered the bar, and was not seen again that day. While, on the other side, Daphne stood cowering against the mahogany casings, looking deadly pale, with great black rings around her eyes.

Percy was quite friendly to Bultishaw, and introduced him to a friend of his in the same regiment, named Prosser, a young man who had previously been in a drapery store. It was not till later in the evening that the dull rumble of some imminent tragedy caused the vast bulk of the linoleum manager's body to tremble.

He had been conscious of it all the afternoon. He was frightened. He did not like the way Percy had asked for Ticknett. He did not like Ticknett's disappearance, and above all he did not like the way Daphne had cowered against the wall. There was something at the back of all this, something uncomfortable. He dreaded things of this nature. Why couldn't people go on quietly, eating and drinking and being comfortable? He avoided "The Duchess of Teck," and actually stayed late at his work and caught up some arrears. He decided to go quickly home. When he got outside he commenced to walk, when suddenly Percy came out of a doorway and took hold of his arm. Bultishaw started.

"What is it? What do you want?" he said.

There was something very curious about Percy. He had never seen him like that before. He had been drinking, but he was not drunk. In fact, Bultishaw had never seen him in some ways so sober, so grimly serious. His lips were trembling, and his eyes were unnaturally bright. He gripped Bultishaw's coat and said:

"Where is your friend Ticknett?"

"I don't know—I haven't seen him since this morning," Bultishaw answered. "Will you swear he isn't in the building? and that you don't know where he IS?"

"Yes," gasped the cork-lino manager.

Percy looked into his eyes for some moments, and then he said queerly: "Ticknett knows that I've got to report first thing in the morning. I've just seen Daphne home. There'll be a packet for Ticknett, do you see? I say there'll be a packet for him. D' you understand. Bulky-chops?"

Bultishaw was very frightened. He did not know a bit what the young man meant. He only knew that he wanted to get away. He didn't want to be mixed up in this. He mumbled:

"I see-er-a packet? ... I'll tell him."

"No, you needn't tell him," answered the soldier. "I 'm sayin' this for your benefit. I say there'll be a packet for him. D' you understand? There'll be a packet for him."

And he melted into the night ....

From the day when Percy disappeared with these mysterious words on his lips to the day when the news came that he had been killed there was an interval of time that varied according to the occupation and the preoccupation of his particular acquaintances. To Bultishaw it appeared a very long time, but this may have been partly due to the fact that in the interval he had spent most of the time in bed with a very serious illness. He had been lying on his back, staring at the ceiling, and he had not been allowed to drink. The time had consequently hung very heavily on his hands, and his thoughts had been feeding on each other. The exact time was in effect eleven weeks.

During the latter part of this period his friend Ticknett paid him many visits, and had been very kind and attentive. And it was he indeed who brought the news that Percy had been killed.

It was one evening when it was nearly dark, and Bultishaw was sitting up in his dressing-gown in front of the fire, and his daughter Elsie was sitting on the other side of the fireplace, sewing.

Ticknett paid one of his customary visits. Elsie showed him to an easy chair between the two, and after Ticknett's solicitous enquiries regarding Bultishaw's health, the two men reverted to their usual discussion of the staff of Cotterway's and their friends. Suddenly Ticknett remarked quite casually:

"Oh, by the way, young Percy has been killed at the front."

And then the room seemed to become violently darker. Bultishaw struggled to frame some suitable comment upon this but the words failed to come. He sat there with his fat, puffy hands pressing the sides of his easy chair. At last he said:

"Elsie, you might go and get my beef-tea ready."

When his daughter had gone out of the room, he still had nothing to say. He had not dismissed her for the purpose of speaking about the matter to Ticknett, but simply because a strange mood had come to him that he could not trust himself. In the gathering darkness he could see the sallow mask of his friend's face looking at the fire, and his cold eyes peering beneath his heavy brows. Bultishaw at length managed to say:

"Any particulars?" And Ticknett replied:

"No. It was in the papers yesterday." And then Ticknett smiled and added:

"So you won't have to bother about your job any longer, Mr. Bultishaw." And Bultishaw thought: "There'll be a packet for you, Ticknett. A packet. Do you understand? And by God! you'll deserve it!"

He was still uncertain of what "the packet" would contain, but he had thought a lot about it during his illness, and he was sure the packet would contain something unpleasant, if not terrible. And yet Ticknett was his friend, in fact his only friend; the man who had saved him in a crisis, and who waited on him in his sickness. He tried to pull himself together, and he managed to say in his normally wheezy voice: "I hope to be back next week." And indeed on the following Tuesday he did once more report himself to the heads of the firm. He was still very weak and ill, and the doctor had warned him to avoid alcohol in any form. But by half past twelve he felt so exhausted he decided that a little whisky and milk might help to get him through the day. He crawled round to "The Duchess of Teck" and was soon amongst his congenial acquaintants. It was very warm, very pleasant and ingratiating, the atmosphere of the bar. He ordered his whisky and milk, and then became aware of a striking vacancy. Daphne was not there. Mrs. Clarke and Gladys were busy serving drinks, and a tall thin girl was helping them. A peculiar sense of misgiving came to Bultishaw.

He did not like to say anything about it to Mrs. Clarke, but he turned to an old habitue, named Benjamin Strigge, and he whispered:

"Where's Daphne to-day, Mr. Strigge?" And Mr. Strigge answered:

"Daphne? She ain't been here for nearly three months. There was some story about her and young Percy. I've really forgotten what it was all about. Of course, you've been away, Mr. Bultishaw. You've missed all the spicy news, eh? They never interest me. Ha, ha, ha! Can I order you another whisky and milk?" Bultishaw declined with thanks, and stood there sucking his pipe. In a few minutes Ticknett entered the bar. He appeared to be quite cheerful, and for him garrulous. He was very solicitous about Bultishaw's health, and insistent that he should not stand near a draught. He talked optimistically about the war, and Bultishaw replied in monosyllables. And all the time the ridiculous thought kept racing through his mind:

"You're going to get a packet, my friend."

It was a week later that Prosser turned up. He was one of eleven men, the sole survivors of a regiment-Percy's regiment. Prosser was slightly wounded in the foot, and strangely altered. He stammered and was no longer a gay companion. He had a wild, abstracted look, as though he had lost the power of listening, and was entirely occupied with inner visions. They could get little information out of him about Percy. He described certain scenes and experiences very vividly, but the description did not convey much to most of the men, for the reason that they were entirely devoid of imagination. The regiment had, as a matter of fact, been ambushed, and practically annihilated. A mine had done some deadly work. He had seen Percy and another man come into the lines in the morning. It was just daybreak. They had been on listening patrol. He had seen them both making their way along a trench to a dug-out, to the very spot where five minutes later the mine blew up.

"Didn't you never see Percy again?" some one asked. "No," answered the warrior. "But I 'eard 'im laugh." "Laugh!"

"Yes. You know the way he used to laugh. Loud and clear-like. He must have been two hundred yards away. Suddenly he laughed, and I says to Peters, who was on my right, "Ark at that blighter, Percy! Seems to think even this is amusin" I'adn't got the words out of my mouth when ... just as though the whole bally earth had burst into a gas ... not a quarter of a mile away-thought I was gone myself right over in the quarter where Percy had gone ... thousands of tons of mud flung up into the sky, ... you could 'ear the earth being ripped to pieces, and there were men in it .... Oh, Gawd!"

Bultishaw shuddered and felt faint, and the rest of the company seemed to think they were hearing a rather highly colored account of some quite inconceivable phenomenon. Prosser was further detailing his narrative, when he happened to drop a phrase that was very illuminating to Bultishaw. He was speaking of another man some of them knew, named Bates. The phrase he used was: "Charley Bates got a packet too!" A packet! Bultishaw paid for his drink and went out into the street. He felt rather hot and cold round the temples. He took a cab home, and went straight to bed, explaining to his daughters that he had had" a very heavy day." When he rolled between the sheets the true meaning of that sinister phrase "getting a packet kept revolving through his mind. It was evidently the military expression, and very terse and grim and sardonic it was. These men who met a violent end "got a packet." Percy had got a packet. Bates had got a packet, but why should Ticknett, dividing his days between a furnishing house and a saloon bar, get a packet? It was incredible, preposterous. Men who went out to fight for their country, well-they might expect it. But not men who lead simple, honest, commercial lives. If Ticknett got a packet, why should he not himself get a packet? He passed a sleepless night, but there was one problem he determined to try and solve on the morrow.

Somehow Bultishaw could not bring him-self to ask Mrs. Clarke about Daphne, and Gladys, whom he always suspected of laughing at him, he would certainly not question. He eventually got her address from a potman, who had carried some of her things home for her.

When he did get her address, it took him over a week to make up his mind to visit her. He thumbed the envelope and breathed heavily on it, put it back in his pocket and took it out again, and tried to dismiss it from his mind, but the very touch of it seemed to burn his body. At length, on the following Saturday night, he tucked it finally into his waistcoat pocket, and set out in the direction of Kilburn.

It was very dark when he found the obscure street. And the number of the address was a gaunt house of four stories above a low-class restaurant where sausages and slabs of fish were frying in the window, to tempt hungry passers-by. He stumbled up the dark stairs, and was told by two children whom he could not see that "Miss Allen" lived on the third floor. He rang the wrong bell on the third floor (there were two lots of inhabitants) and was told by a lady that "she liked his bleeding cheek waking her in her first sleep, ringing the wrong bell," and the door was slammed in his face.

He tried the other bell, and the door was opened immediately by a gaunt woman who said:

"Who's that? Oh, I thought it was the doctor!"

Bultishaw asked if Miss Daphne Allen lived there, and gave his own name. The woman stared at him and then said:

"Wait a minute."

She shut the door and left him outside. After a time she came back and said: "What do you want?" Bultishaw said, "I just want to speak to her for a few minutes."

The woman again retired, and left him for nearly five minutes. He stood there shivering with cold on the stone stairs, and listening to the strange mixture of noises: children quarreling in the street below, and in the room opposite some one playing a mouth organ. At last the woman came back.
She said:

"Come in."

He followed her into a poky room, dimly lighted by a tin paraffin lamp with a pink glass. In the comer of the room was a bed on which a woman was lying, feeding a baby. Her face looked white and thin and her hair was bound up in a shawl. It was Daphne. She looked at him listlessly, and said:

"Well, have you brought any money from him!"

Bultishaw stood blinking at her, unable to comprehend. Whom did she mean by "him"! He coughed, and tried to formulate some sympathetic enquiry, when suddenly the gaunt woman who had shown him in turned on him and cried:

"Well, what the hell are you standing there like that for! You've come from him, I suppose? You're 'is greatest pal, ain't yer! We've never seen a farthing of 'is money yet since the dirty blackguard did 'er in. What 'ave you come slobbering up 'ere for, if it ain't to bring some money! The b-y 'ound! If it 'adn't been for 'im, she might be the wife of a respectable sowljer, and gettin' 'er maintenance and pension, and all that."

There was a mild sob from the bed, and a pleading voice that cried: "Aunty! Aunty}"

And the baby started to cry. While these little things were happening, the slow-moving mind of Bultishaw for once worked rapidly, came to a conclusion, and formed a resolution. He moved ponderously to the lamp, and took out his purse. He looked across the lamp at Daphne and said: "He sends you this. He's sorry not to have sent before. He ... "

The elder woman dashed toward the table, and looked at the money.

"How much is it?" she said, and then turning to Daphne, she rasped: "It's two quid. That's better than nothing. Is there any more to come?"

Bultishaw again looked at Daphne. She was bending over the child. She seemed indifferent. A strand of her hair had broken loose beneath the shawl. Bultishaw stammered:

"Yes-er-of course. There'll be-er-the same again."

"'Ow often?" whined the elder woman.

"Er-two pounds-every fortnight. Er-I'll bring it myself. "

The big man blew his nose, and shuffled from one foot to another. "Are you getting better? Is there anything else?" he mumbled.

"Oh, no" whined the elder woman. "We're living in the lap of luxury. Everything we could want. Ain't we, Cissy?"

The woman on the bed did not answer, and Bultishaw fumbled his way out of the room.

That night Bultishaw had a mild return of his illness. He was very feverish. His mind became occupied with visions of Percy. Percy, the gay, the debonair. There was a long line of poplars by a canal, and some low buildings of a factory on the left. The earth was seamed with jagged cuts and holes. Men were burrowing their way underground like moles. The thing was like a torn fringe of humanity, wildly insane. It was very dark, but one was conscious that vast numbers of men were scratching their way toward each other, zigzagging in a drunken, frenzied manner. There was a stench of decaying matter, and of some chemical even more penetrating. There were millions and millions of men, but they were all invisible, silently scratching and listening. Suddenly amidst the dead silence there was the loud burst of Percy's laughter-just as he had laughed in the bar of "The Duchess of Teck" -and his voice rang through the night:

"Hullo! hullo! HULLO! So here we all are!"

And this challenge seemed to awaken the lurking passions of the night. Bultishaw groaned and started up in bed, and cried out:

"O God! a thousand tons of mud! a thousand tons of mud!"

On the following day Bultishaw made a grievous mistake in his accounts. He was severely hauled over the coals by the directors. As the weeks proceeded he made other mistakes. He became morose and abstracted. He drank his whisky with less and less soda, till he was drinking it almost neat.

"Old Bulky-chops's brain's going" said some of the other salesmen.

He would lean up against the bar, and h stare at Ticknett. Their old conversational relationship became reversed. It was Bultishaw who listened, and Ticknett who did the talking. The soft goods manager appeared to be in excellent trim at the time. He seemed more light-hearted than he had been for years. He spoke in his quiet voice about the tactics of Russian generals and the need for general compulsion in this country for everybody up to the age of forty-five (Ticknett was forty-seven). At Christmas-time he sent Bultishaw a case of old port wine. His position in the firm became more assured. It was said that Ticknett had bought a large block of shares in Cotterway's, Limited, and that he stood a good chance of being put on the board of directorship.

And Bultishaw watched his upward progress with a curious intentness. He himself was blundering down the hill. He had made a large inroad into his capital, and the day could not be far distant when he would be dismissed. Every fortnight he went out to Kilburn and took two sovereigns, and he never spoke of this to Ticknett.

Elsie Bultishaw was very mysterious. In her black crepe dress she bustled about the small room, holding the teapot in her hand.

"They say you should never speak ill of the dead," she whispered to her visitor. She emptied a packet of tea into a caddy, and tipped three teaspoonsful into the pot.

"Of course," she continued, "It's very hard on me and Dorothy. It's lucky Dorothy's got that job at the War Office, or I don't know what we'd do."

"Your pore father was not a careful man, I know, my dear," said the visitor. Elsie poured the boiling water on to the tea-leaves, and sighed.

"It wasn't only that, my pear," she answered. She coughed and then added in a low voice:

"There was some woman in the case. A barmaid, in fact. Of course, pore father's illness cost a lot of money, what with doctors, and specialists, and loss of time and that. But it seems he'd been keeping this woman too, taking her money every fortnight. When everything's settled up, there won't be more 'n twenty pounds a year for me and Dorothy."

"Dear, dear!" said the visitor. "It's all very tragic, my dear."'

"You can't think," Elsie continued, warming to the excitement of her narrative, "what we've been through. We could never have lived through it, if it hadn't been for Mr. Ticknett. He's been kindness itself. And such an extraordinary hallucination pore father had about him, I didn't tell you, did I, dear!'

"No, dear."

"I'll never forget that night father came home. He'd been drinking, of course. But it wasn't only that. I've never seen him like it. He just raved. It was very late, and me and Dorothy were going to bed. He came stumbling into this room, his eyes lookin' all bright and glassylike. He started by saying that the dead could speak. He said he'd only obeyed the voice of the dead. And then he said something about a packet, and about Mr. Ticknett. I was terrified. He described something he said he'd just done. He walked about the room. He pointed to that corner.

'Look,' he says, 'Ticknett was stand-in' there.' There'd been a dinner to celebrate Mr. Ticknett's election on to the board of directors of Cotterway's. 'I never take my eyes off him all the evening,' father says. ' It was after the dinner, and we went into the saloon. Ticknett was surrounded by his friends. I watched his lying, treacherous, yellow face smirkin' all around. And suddenly a voice spoke to me, a voice from some dim field in France. It says, "Ticknett's going to have a packet." And then I drew my revolver and shot him through the face!' Dorothy shrieked, and I tried to get father to bed. Of course it was all rubbish. He'd never shot no one. It was just raving. Everybody knows that Mr. Ticknett's been father's best friend. He's helped him crowds of times. A nicer man you couldn't meet. He's coming to tea on Sunday. We managed to get poor father to bed, and to get a doctor. But it was no good. He babbled like a child all night. It was so funny like. He really was like a child. He kept on repeating, 'A thousand tons of mud!' and then suddenly, about mornin', he got quite quiet, and his face looked like some great baby's lying there ... He died quite peaceful."

Elsie performed a little mild weep, and the visitor indulged in various exclamations of sympathy and interest.

"Oh, dear," she concluded, "it's dreadful the things people imagine when they're like that."

Elsie went over all the details again, and the visitor recounted a tragic episode she had heard of in connection with a corporal's widow, who was a relation of her own landlady. They discussed the dreadful war, and its effect on the price of bacon and margarine.

After her departure, Elsie washed out and ironed some handkerchiefs, and then prepared her sister's supper. Dorothy arrived home about seven, and the two sisters discussed the events of the day. They sat in front of the fire and listened to a pot stewing. At a sudden pause, Dorothy looked into the fire, and said:

"Do you think Ticknett's really keen on me, Elsie r' Elsie giggled, and kissed her sister.

"You'd have to be blind not to see that," she said; and then she whispered:

"Are you really keen on him?"

The younger sister continued staring into the fire.

"I don't know. I think I am. I-Isn't this stew nearly done?"

Elsie again giggled, and proceeded to dish up the stew. Before this operation was completed, there was a knock at the door.

Elsie said, "Oh, curse!" and went, and opened it.

In the doorway stood a woman with a small parcel. Her face was deadly white and her lips colorless. She looked like a woman to whom everything that could hap- pen had happened long ago, and the result had left her lifeless and indifferent. She said listlessly:

"Are you Miss Bultishaw?"

And Elsie said, "Yes"

The woman entered, and looked round the room.

"May I speak to you a moment? Is this your sister?" she said. Elsie answered: "Yes; what do you want?" "I want to make an explanation, and to give you some money."

She untied the packet, and placed some notes on to the table-cloth. "What the hell's this?" exclaimed Elsie.

"This is all I could find," muttered the listless woman. "I found them in his breast-pocket. They belonged to your father. It wasn't your father at all who - ought to have paid. He ought to have paid. So I've taken them from him. I hope there's enough. I'm afraid there may not be. It's all I have. It's only-right you should have it."

The two sisters stared at her, and involuntarily drew closer together. It was Dorothy who eventually managed to speak:

"What are you talking about I' ' she said. "Who do you mean by 'him?"

"Ticknett!"

The sisters gasped, and Dorothy gave a little cry.

"Here! what do you mean?" she said breathlessly. "Have you pinched this money from Ticknett? You'd better be careful. He's coming here. We'll have you arrested."

The listless woman shook her head.

"No, no," she said in her toneless voice. "Don't you believe that. He won't come here."

"Why won't he come here?" rasped Dorothy, with a note of challenge.

The strange visitor stood staring vacantly at the fire. She seemed not to have heard. Her lips were trembling. Suddenly she answered in the same dull, lifeless manner:

"Because he's lying on my bed with a bullet through his heart."


In the Way of Business

As the large, thick-set man with the red face, the bushy mustache, and the very square chin swung round on his swivel chair, at the great roll-top desk with its elaborate arrangements of telephones, receivers, and electric buttons, he conveyed to the little mild-eyed man waiting on a chair by the door the sense of infinite power.

And surely it must be a position requiring singular gifts and remarkable capacity. For was this not Dollbones, the house famous throughout the civilized world for supplying trimmings, gimp, embroidery, buttons, and other accessories to nearly every retail furnisher in England and the colonies? and was not this Mr. Godfrey Hylam, the London manager? To hold such a position a man must have not only brains, and an infinite capacity for work and driving power, but he must have character, a genius for judging people and making quick decisions.

"Almost like a general," thought the mild-eyed man by the door. He had waited fifty minutes in the outer office for his interview, and on being at length shown in, had been told to "sit down a minute." This minute had been protracted into thirty-five minutes, but it was very interesting to watch the great man grappling with the myriad affairs that came whispering through the wires, and giving sharp instructions to the two flurried clerks who sat in the same office, or dictating to the young lady stenographer who sat furtively on a small chair by his side scribbling into a book with a fountain-pen.

"She looks ill and worried," thought the little man. He was indulging in a dreamy speculation on the girl's home life, when he was suddenly pulled up by the percussion of Mr. Hylam's voice. He realized that the great man was speaking to him. He was saying:

"Let's see, what's your name?"

"Thomas Pinwell, sir," he answered, and stood up. "What name?" repeated the big man.

"Pinwell-Thomas Pinwell," he said in a rather louder voice.

Mr. Hylam looked irritably among some papers and sighed. He then continued dictating a letter to the stenographer. When that was finished he got up, and went out of the room. He was absent about ten minutes, and then came hurrying in with some more papers. He called out as he walked:

"Jackson, have you got that statement from Jorrocks, Musgrove & Bellwither?"

One of the clerks jumped up and said: "I'll find it, sir."

The clerk took some time to do this, and in the meanwhile Mr. Hylam dictated another report to the young lady. Then the clerk brought the statement, and he and Mr. Hylam discussed it at some length. He gave the clerk some further instructions, which were twice interrupted by the telephone bell. When this was finished, Mr. Hylam again caught sight of the little man by the door. He looked at him with surprise, and said:

"Let's see, what's your name?"

"Pinwell-Thomas Pinwell, sir," he answered patiently.

Mr. Hylam again sighed and fingered a lot of papers in pigeon-holes. At that moment there was a knock, and a boy in buttons entered and said:

"There's Mr. Curtis, of Curtis, Tonks & Curtis, called."

"Oh!" exclaimed Mr. Hylam. "Yes. All right. Er-ask him to come in. I want to see him." He turned to the telephone, and asked someone to put him on to someone else, and while waiting with the receiver to his ear, his eye once more caught sight of the little man by the door. He called out to him:

"Oh!-er-just wait outside a minute, Mr.—er—Hullo! is that you, Thomson?"

Finding himself temporarily dismissed, Mr. Pinwell took up his hat and went into the outer office. There was a tall, elderly man with a fur-lined overcoat standing there, and he was immediately shown in. He remained with Mr. Hylam just one hour. At the end of that time, one of the directors called and went out to lunch with Mr. Hylam. A clerk gave Mr. Pinwell the tip that he had better call back about four O'clock. He said he would do so. He had had thirty years' experience in the furnishing trade, and he knew that "business was business" One had to be patient, to conform to its prescripts. A gentleman like Mr. Hylam lived under continual pressure. He was acting according to his conscience in the best interests of the firm. One had to take one's chance with him. After all, it would be very nice to get the job. He had been out so long, and he was not so young as he used to be. He thought of his placid wife and the two children. They were indeed getting into a very penurious state. He understood that the salary would be thirty shillings per week and a small royalty on the sales. Not a princely emolument but it would make all the difference. Besides, what might not the royalties amount to? If he worked hard and energetically he might make between two and three pounds per week who knows? He went into an aerated bread shop and had a cup of tea and a piece of seed cake and read the morning paper. He stayed there as long as he dare, and then went for a stroll round the streets. At four o 'clock precisely he presented himself at the managerial office at Dollbones once more. Mr. Hylam had not returned. They expected him every minute. There were five other people waiting to see him. At half-past four Mr. Hylam came in, smoking a cigar. He was accompanied by another gentleman. They walked right through the waiting crowd and went into the inner office and shut the door. As a matter of fact, Mr, Pinwell did not see the manager at all that day. So great was the congestion of business in the trimming, gimp, embroidery, and button business that afternoon that he was advised by one of the least aggressive clerks, at about a quarter to six, to try his luck in the morning. It was a quarter-past three on the following afternoon that he eventually obtained his interview with Mr. Hylam, and it was from his point of view entirely satisfactory. Mr. Hylam said:

"Let's see. You told me your name?"

"Yes, sir," he answered." Thomas Pinwell."

Mr. Hylam seemed at last to find the papers he desired. He said: "Er-just come here. Show me your references."

Mr. Pinwell approached the great desk deferentially. On it was a chart of London with one section shaded red. Mr. Hylam read the references carefully and then asked one or two searching questions. At last he said:

"Well, now, look here. This is your section. Go to Mr. Green, and he will give you the cards and samples. Then go to Rodney in the Outer London department upstairs, and he will give you a list of several hundred furnishing houses with the names of the buyers and a few particulars. Everything else you must find out. The salary is thirty shillings a week and two per cent, on sales completed. Settlement monthly. Good-day, Mr.—er—"

He turned to the telephone, and Mr. Pin-well's heart beat rapidly. He had really got a job again! As he walked to the door he had a vision of the expression of delight on his wife's face as he told her the news. He visualized a certain day in a certain month when he would bring home a lot of sovereigns and buy the children things. Two per cent.! For every hundred pounds' worth of orders, two golden sovereigns of his very own! It seemed too good to be true!

His wife indeed did share with him the comforting joys of this new vista of commercial prosperity. They occupied now two rooms in Camling Town, and Tom had been out so long there was no immediate prospect of a removal. But the rent was now secure and just the barest necessities of life, and everything depended on the two per cent, commission. He was to start on the following Monday, and the intervening days were filled with active preparations. There were shirts to mend, an overcoat to be stitched, a pair of boots to have the heels set up, and three new collars to be bought. These were vital things pertinent to the active propaganda of the bread-winner. Other things were urgent, -a new piece of oil-cloth for the bedroom, some underclothes for the girls, and several small debts-but all these things could wait, at any rate a month or two, till the commissions started coming in. For Mrs. Pinwell herself there never seemed necessities. She always managed to look somehow respectable, and, as Mr. Pinwell once remarked to a neighbor," My wife is a marvel, sir, with a string bag. She always believes in bringing the things home herself. She goes out into the High Street, Camling Town, on a Saturday night, and I assure you, sir, it's surprising what she will bring back. She will make a shilling go further than many of them would half-a-crown. She is a remarkable woman. It surprises me how she manages to bargain, being so unassuming, so diffident, as it were, in the home."

There was nothing, then, missing in the necessary equipment of Mr. Pinwell as he set out with his leather case of samples on the following Monday. It was a cold, bright day, and he enjoyed the exercise of walking. He was not by nature a pushful man and he found the business of calling on people whom he did not know somewhat irksome. Fortunately he was by temperament patient and understanding, and he made allowances when people were rude to him, or kept him waiting indefinitely and then gave him no orders. "It's all in the way of business," he thought as he shuffled out of the shop and sought the next street.

At the end of the first week he explained to his wife:

"You see, my dear, there's a lot of spade-work to be done yet. I 'm afraid Flinders, who had the round before me, must have neglected it disgracefully. It all requires working up again. One has to get to know people, the right people, of course. They seem prejudiced against one like, at first.

"Was that Mr. Flinders who used to—" began Mrs. Pinwell in a whisper.

"Yes, my dear, I 'm afraid he drank. It was a very distressing story, very distressing indeed. They say he drank himself to death. A very clever salesman too-very clever! They tell me he worked this district up splendidly, and then gradually let it go to pieces."

"Dear, dear! I can't think how people do such things!" murmured Mrs. Pin well.

"It was a great recommendation in my case," continued her husband, "that I was a teetotaler. Mr. Hylam made a great point of that. He asked me several times, and read the letter of Judkins & Co. vouching for my honesty and sobriety for a period of twenty-two years. He seemed very pleased about that."

At the end of the first month the orders that Mr. Pinwell had secured for Doll bones were of a negligible character. He felt discouraged—as though conscious of there being something fundamentally wrong in his method of doing business but his wife cheered him by expressing her view that it would probably take months before his initial spade-work would take effect.

He started on his rounds a little earlier after that, and stayed a little later. He became more persistent and more patient. He went back again and again to see people who seemed inaccessible. He tried to be a little more assertive and plausible in his solicitations, but at the end of the second month there was little improvement in his returns, and his commissions amounted to scarcely enough to pay for the new oil-cloth in the sitting-room.

The optimism of Mrs. Pinwell was in no way affected by this failure, but a more alarming note was struck by Mr. Rodney of the "Outer London Department." He told Mr. Pinwell that Mr. Hylam was not at all satisfied with his work so far, and he would have to show greater energy and enterprise during the ensuing month, or the firm would be impelled to try a new traveler for that district, one who could show better results.

Mr. Pinwell was very alarmed. The idea of being "out" again kept him awake at night. It was a very serious thing. He put in longer hours still, and hurried more rapidly between his calls. He increased his stock of samples till they amounted to a very considerable weight. He made desperate appeals for orders, ringing the changes on various ways of expressing himself. But at the end of the next week there was still no improvement on the pages of his order-book. There was one firm in particular who caused him considerable heartburning—Messrs. Carron and Musswell. These were quite the biggest people in the neighborhood, and had five different branches, each doing a prosperous business. Mr. Pinwell for the life of him could not find out how to get into the good graces of this firm. No one seemed to know who bought for them, and he was referred from one person to another, and sent dashing from one branch to another, all to no purpose.

He had one friend who had a small retail business of his own, a Baptist named Senner, who gave him small orders occasionally. He went into Mr. Senner's shop one Friday, and feeling thoroughly tired and discouraged, he poured out his tale of woe to Mr. Senner. Mr. Senner was a large doleful man, to whom the sorrows of others were as balm. He listened to Mr. Pin-well's misfortunes in sympathetic silence, breathing heavily. At the end of the peroration his son entered the shop. He was a white-faced, dissipated-looking young man who wore lavender ties and brushed his hair back.

One might have imagined that he would have been a source of disappointment to Mr. Senner, but quite the contrary was the case. The son had a genius for concealing his vices from his father, and his father had a great opinion of the boy's intelligence and character. He certainly had a faculty of securing orders for his father's business.

On this occasion Mr. Senner turned to his son and said: "Harry, who buys for Carron & Musswell!" The son looked at Mr. Pinwell and fidgeted with his nails. Then he grinned weakly and said:

"Oh, you want to get hold of Clappe." Mr. Pinwell came forward and said:

"Oh, indeed! I 'm really very much obliged to you. It's very kind! Mr. Clappe, you say? Dear me! yes. Thank you very much. I'll go and ask for Mr. Clappe."

And he shook the young man's hand.

The young man continued grinning in rather a superior manner, and at that moment Mr. Senner's attention was attracted by a customer who entered the shop. Mr. Pinwell picked up his bags and went out. He had not gone more than a dozen yards when he became aware of Senner junior at his side. The young man still grinned, and he said:

"I say, you know, it's no good your going to Carron & Musswell's and asking for Clappe. You'll never get hold of him in that way"

"Really!" exclaimed Mr. Pinwell. "Now tell me, what would you suggest!"

The young man sniffed and looked up and down the street, and a curiously leery expression came over his face. Then he said:

"I expect I could fix it for you all right, Pinwell. You'd better come with me into the bar of the ' Three Amazons' after lunch. I'll introduce you. Of course, you know, Mr. Pinwell,—er—you know, business is business. We always like to oblige our friends, and so on-"

He looked at Mr. Pinwell furtively and bit his nails. For the moment Mr. Pin well could not catch the drift of these smiles and suggestions, but he had been in the upholstery line for twenty-seven years, and it suddenly dawned upon him that of course the young man was suggesting that if he introduced him, and business came out of it, he would expect a commission or a bonus. He was quite reasonable. He had a sort of ingrained repugnance to these things himself, but he knew that it was done in business. It was quite a usual thing. Some of the best firms- He took the young man's hand and said:

"Er-of course Mr. Senner, I shall be very pleased to accommodate you. It's -er-only natural, only natural of course. Business is business. Where shall I meet you?"

The appointment was made for the corner of Mulberry Road at half-past two; and at that hour Mr. Pinwell arrived with two heavily laden bags. He walked by the side of the young man down the street, and then crossed over into the High Road. Eight opposite them was a large gaudy public house called "The Three Amazons" and they crossed over to it. A feeling of diffidence and shyness came over Mr. Pinwell. He had only entered a public house on about three occasions in his life, and then under some very stringent business demands, or else to get a bottle of brandy when his wife was very ill.

Nevertheless he followed the young man through a passage and entered the saloon bar, in the corner of which he deposited his bags. The bar was fairly crowded with business men, but there was one figure that by its personality immediately arrested Mr. Pinwell's attention. He was a very big man in a new shiny top-hat with a curl to it. He was leaning heavily against the center of the bar, and was surrounded by three or four other men who seemed to be hanging on his words. He had a large red face and small, dark, expressionless eyes. The skin seemed to be tight and moist, and to bind up his features in inelastic bags, except round the eyes, where it puckered up into dark yellowish layers of flesh. His hands were fat and stiff and blue like the hands of a gouty subject. His gray hair curled slightly under the brim of his hat, and his clothes were ponderously impressive from the silk reveres of his tail coat to the dark-brown spats that covered his square-toed boots. As they entered, this impressive individual looked in their direction and gave young Mr. Senner a faint nod, and then continued his conversation.

"That's Clappe," whispered Mr. Pin-well's cicerone, and dusted the knees of his trousers. He then added:

"We'd better wait a bit."

They stood there in the comer of the bar, and the young man produced a silver cigarette-case and offered its contents to Mr. Pinwell, an overt act of kindness which that gentleman appreciated but did not take advantage of. They waited there twenty minutes before an opportunity presented itself of making any approach to the great man. But in the meantime Mr. Pinwell watched the conversation with considerable interest. The four men stood very close together, smoking, and speaking in thick whispers. He was alarmed at moments by the way in which one would hold a glass of whisky-and-water at a perilous angle over the waistcoat of another, while fumbling with a cigarette in the unoccupied hand. He could not hear the conversation, but occasional sentences reached him: "It's the cheapest line there is." "Here! I tell you where you can get—" "D'you know what they paid last year?"

"I 'ad 'im by the short 'airs that time." "'E says to me—"

It occurred to Mr. Pinwell that there was something distressing about this scene, something repelling and distasteful, but he consoled himself with the reflection that after all business had to be conducted somehow. Money had to be made to pay for the streets and the lamp-posts, and the public baths and the battleships. "Business is not always pleasant," he reflected, "but it has to be done."

At the end of twenty minutes two of the men went away and left Mr. Clappe talking apathetically to the remaining man.

"Now's our chance," said Senner junior, and he walked across the bar. He seized on a lull in the conversation to step forward and touch Mr. Clappe on the arm.

"Er-excuse me, Mr. Clappe," he said. "This is my friend Mr. Pinwell, of Dollbones. "

The big man glanced from Senner junior to Mr. Pinwell and gave that gentleman an almost imperceptible nod. He then sighed, breathed heavily, and took a long drink from the glass in front of him.

"I'm very pleased to meet you, Mr. Clappe," said Pinwell nervously. "I've heard about you. I 'm with Dollbones, you know, the Dollbones. We have-er—several very good lines just now."

The great Clappe fixed him with his lugubrious eyes and suddenly said in a thick voice:

"What'll you drink?"

It is curious that Mr. Pinwell with all his experience should have been taken back by this hospitable request. He stammered and said:

"Oh! thank you very much, sir. I don't think I'll-at least, I'll have-er-a lime-juice and soda."

And then Mr. Clappe behaved in a very extraordinary way. An expression of utter, dejection came over his face. He puffed his cheeks out and suddenly muttered" Oh, my God!"

And then he rolled round and deliberately turned his back on Mr. Pinwell and his friend! It was a very trying moment. Mr. Pinwell was at his wit's end how to act, and Senner junior did not help him in any way. On the contrary he seemed to be taking Mr. Clappe's side. He gave a sort of snigger of disgust, and called across the bar in a jaunty voice:

"Johnny Walker and soda, please, Miss Parritt."

Mr. Pinwell gaped ineffectually at the back of the great man, and hesitated whether to make any further advance. But he was relieved of the necessity of coming to a decision by the act of Mr. Clappe himself, who slowly drained the remnants of refreshment in his glass, and then walked heavily out of the bar, without looking round.

In the meantime young Senner had acquired his drink, and was feverishly tapping the end of a cigarette on the rail. He took a long drink and spluttered slightly, and then, turning on Mr. Pinwell, he said:

"What particular brand of blankety fool are you?"

"I beg your pardon?" exclaimed Mr. Pinwell, amazed.

"I tell you," said the young man, "you're a particular type of blankety fool. You've missed the chance of yer life I Don't you know when a man like Clappe asks yer to have a drink yer a blankety fool not to? D' you know that man places thousands and thousands of pounds a year for Carron & Musswell? Thousands, I tell yer! It don't matter to 'im where he places the orders. He puts it all out among 'is pals. You 'ad a chance of being a pal, and you've muffed it!"

"But—but—but—" spluttered Mr. Pin-well." I really—I—had no idea. I said I would have a drink. It was only that I ordered a—er—non-alcoholic drink. I really can't—"

"Psaugh!"

Young Mr. Senner swirled the whisky round in his glass and drank it at a gulp. Then he muttered: "Gawd! Asking Clappe for a lime-juice and soda!"

Mr. Pinwell thought about this meditatively. He wondered whether he had been in the wrong. After all, people all had their notions of the way to conduct business. Business was a very big thing. It had "evolved"—that was the word!—evolved out of all sorts of complicated social conditions, supply and demand, and so on. A man perhaps who had been in the habit of taking alcoholic refreshment and expecting others to—it might perhaps be difficult for him to understand.

"Don't you never drink!" suddenly exclaimed Mr. Senner.

"I—er—occasionally have a glass of stout," murmured Mr. Pinwell. "Last Christmas my wife's sister brought us a bottle of canary sac. I have no particular taste for—er—things of this sort-"

"Anyway," said Mr. Senner, "you're not under any bally pledge?"

"Oh, dear me, no!" exclaimed Mr. Pin-well.

"Well, then," answered his youthful adviser. "I should advise you next time Clappe or any one like him asks you to have a drink, lap it up like a poodle and stand him a quick one in return."

Mr. Pinwell surveyed his friend over the rim of his glasses, and thought for some minutes. Then he said:

"I 'm afraid Mr. Clappe is not likely to ask me to have a drink again." But the young man of precocious experience answered:

"If you come in here to-morrer, I'll bet yer he'll have forgotten who you are"

It was all a very astounding experience, and that night in- bed Mr. Pinwell gave the matter long and serious consideration. If his circumstances had been normal he would have hardly thought about it for five consecutive minutes, but his circumstances were anything but normal. They were somewhat desperate. He was on his last month's trial. If he should be out again! ... Both the children wanted new clothes, and Eileen's boots were all to pieces. And then there was that bill of Batson's for three pounds seventeen shillings, for which payment was demanded by the seventeenth; there were other bills less urgent perhaps but-the little man kept turning restlessly in bed and even in his sleep he made febrile calculations.

It must be acknowledged that the result of Mr. Pinwell's nocturnal meditations tended to loosen certain moral tendencies in himself. He set out on the morrow in a peculiarly equivocal frame of mind, wavering between conflicting impulses, but already predisposed to temporize with his conscience if by so doing he could advance what he considered to be the larger issues of business considerations. These first concessions, curiously enough, were not made at the instance of the great Mr. Clappe, however, but at that of a certain Mr. Cherish whom he met during that day. He was a breezy, amiable person, and the manager of the International Hardwood Company. He was just going out to lunch as Mr. Pinwell called, and being in a particularly buoyant mood, owing to a successful business deal, he took hold of our hero's arm and drew him into the street. As they walked along he asked what it was that Pinwell wanted, and that gentleman immediately expatiated on the virtues of the goods he had at his disposal. While talking he found himself almost unconsciously led into the bar of a public-house called "The Queen of Roumania." And when asked by Mr. Cherish," What he was going to have," a sudden desperate instinct of adventure came over him, and he called for whisky. When it was brought he drank it in little sips, and thought it the most detestable drink he had ever tasted. But he determined to see the matter through, and salved his conscience with the reflection that it was just 'an the way of business." He certainly had to acknowledge that after drinking it he felt a certain elevated sense of assurance. He talked to Mr. Cherish quite unselfconsciously and listened to him with concentrated attention. This mental attitude was quickened by the discovery that Mr. Cherish was actually in need of certain embroideries that Dollbones were in a position to supply. It would be quite a big order. He promised to bring samples of the embroideries on the following day, and took his departure. During the afternoon he felt a sudden reaction from the whisky and was very tired. He went home early, complaining to his wife of a bad headache, as though something had disagreed with him."

Nevertheless the prospect of securing the order for the embroideries excited him considerably, and he went so far as to tell her that he hoped things were soon going to take a tum for the better. He arrived at his appointment the next day to the minute, carrying a very heavy valise stuffed with machine embroideries. He was kept waiting by Mr. Cherish for nearly an hour, and was then ushered into his presence. Mr. Cherish was still in a very jovial mood and had another gentleman with him. He shook Mr. Pinwell's hand and immediately told him three obscene stories that he had just heard-Mr. Cherish was reputed to have the largest repertoire of obscene stories in the trade-and the other gentleman also told two. Pinwell laughed at them to the best of his ability, although they did not appear to him to be particularly humorous. He then felt peculiarly uncomfortable in that for the life of him he could not think of a story in reply. He never could remember these stories. So he opened his valise and displayed the tapestries. The other two gentlemen took a desultory interest in them as tapestries, but a rapacious interest in them as regards value. They were figured tapestries and the price was four pounds seventeen and sixpence a yard. Mr. Cherish mentioned casually that they would want about seventy yards. And then Mr. Pin-well made the rapidest mental calculation he had ever made in his life. Seventy yards at £4,17s. 6d. would be £341,55s. which, at two per cent, would mean just on seven pounds for himself! It was dazzling! Seven gold sovereigns! However, the order was not yet given. The two gentlemen talked about it at some length, and looked up other quotations. At last Mr. Cherish said:

"Well, I think we'll go and see what the 'Queen of Roumania' has got up her sleeve."

Mr. Pinwell and the other gentleman laughed, and they all went out. Mr. Pin well dreaded the prospect of drinking more whisky, but-seven golden sovereigns! enough to pay that bill of Batson's and to buy the children all the clothes they wanted! He knew in any case the etiquette of the trade, and when they arrived in the resplendent bar it was he who insisted on ordering "three Scotch whiskies and a split soda." On the arrival of these regenerating beverages the other two gentlemen resumed their sequence of improper stories. And it was just after the glasses had been re-charged at the instance of Mr. Cherish that he suddenly recollected a story he had heard nearly twenty years ago. It was a disgusting story, and it had impressed itself on his memory for the reason that it struck him when he heard it as being so incredibly vulgar that he could not understand how any one could appreciate it. But as he neared the end of his second glass of whisky it suddenly flashed into his mind that here was the story that Mr. Cherish and his friend would like. He had by this time arrived at an enviable state of unselfconsciousness, and he told the story as well as he had ever told anything in his life. The result amazed him.

The other two gentlemen roared with laughter, and Mr. Cherish tilted his hat back and slapped his leg.

"Gawd's truth! that's a damn good story, Pinwell!" he cried out several times. Other people came into the bar, and Mr. Pinwell found himself something of a hero. Every one seemed to know Mr. Cherish, and he introduced him, and on several occasions said, "I say, Pinwell, tell Mr. Watson that story about the sea captain."

The story was an unqualified success, and seemed in some way to endear him to Mr. Cherish. That gentleman became more confidential and confiding, and they talked about business.

Mr. Pinwell believed he drank four whiskies-and-sodas that afternoon. In any case, he arrived home feeling very bilious and ill. He told his wife he had felt faint, and had taken some brandy+" Thank heaven," he thought, "she doesn't know the difference in smell between brandy and whisky!" He said he would go to bed at once, he thought, and he kissed her in rather a maudlin fashion, and said he knew she would be glad to hear that he had that afternoon taken an order for £341—that would mean nearly seven pounds to them I Enough to buy clothes for the children and pay Batson's bill; he laughed a little hysterically after that, and rolled into bed.

On the following day he was very unwell and unable to get up, and Mrs. Pinwell wrote to the firm and explained that her husband had got his feet wet on his rounds and had contracted a chill. She also in-closed his order-book.

It was three days before he was well enough to resume his rounds, and then he avoided the company of Mr. Cherish and set out on a pilgrimage to the meaner parts of the district. But the orders there seemed few and far between, and a feeling of depression came over him.

On the 1st of the month he was bidden to the presence of Mr. Rodney. That gentleman said that the firm was still dissatisfied with his efforts, but on the strength of the order he had secured from the International Hardwood Co. they were willing to keep him on for another month's trial. But unless at the end of that time he had secured further orders of a similar nature, he must consider his engagement at an end.

It would be tedious and extremely disconcerting to follow the precise movements of Thomas Pinwell during the ensuing four Weeks. It need only be said that, utterly discouraged by his lonely peregrinations in the paths of honest effort, he eventually once more sought the society of young Mr. Senner and Mr. Cherish. In their company he discovered what might be called "a cheering fluidity." He found that whisky made him so ill that he simply could not drink it, but he drank ale, stout, brandy, and gin. None of these things agreed with him, but he found that by drinking as little as possible and ringing the changes on them he could just manage to keep going. The direct result of this moral defection was that his circle of business acquaintances increased at an enormous rate. He gradually got to know the right place and the right hour to catch the right people. His efforts on behalf of Messrs. Dollbones during the following three months were eminently satisfactory, and his own commissions amounted to no mean sum. Neither was his conscience seriously affected by this change of habit. He considered it an inevitable development of his own active progress '4n the way of business." The very word "business" had a peculiarly mesmerizing effect upon him. It was a fetish. He looked upon it as an acolyte might look upon the dogma of some faith he blindly believed in.

He believed that people were in some mysterious way pale adjuncts to the idea that whatever happens," Business" must go on. He would stand in the corner of the bar of "The Queen of Boumania" and look across the street at the Camling Town public wash-houses, a mid-Victorian Gothic building in stucco and red brick, and then, turning his mild watery eyes towards Senner junior, he would say:

"It's a wonderful thing-business, you know, Mr. Senner, a very wonderful thing indeed. Now look at the wash-houses!

They simply have been the result of business. No progress is made, nothing is done except through business. If it weren't for business we should all be Barbarians." And then he would take a little sip at the gin-and-water in front of him.

After copious trials he found that gin affected him less than any of the other drinks, so he stuck to that. He did not like it, but he found that people simply would not do business with him in Camling Town unless he drank and stood drinks. It was very trying, and the most trying part was the necessity of concealing these aberrations from his wife. When he first started he was conscious that he often returned home smelling of the disgusting stuff. He tried cloves, but they were not very effective. Then one day he had a brilliant inspiration. He was unwell again. It happened very often now-at least once a week-and the doctor gave him some medicine. Then it occurred to him that medicine might smell like anything else. He would keep up the medicine. His wife was very unsuspecting. He hated deceiving her. He had never deceived her about anything, but he thought, "Women don't understand business. It is for her benefit that I take it."

Sunday was a great joy to him. He would take the children out for a walk in the morning while his wife cooked the dinner. In the afternoon he would have a nap; but the greatest luxury of the day seemed to him that he need drink nothing except water.

At the end of six months there came a proud day when Mr. Rodney informed him that Mr. Hylam was quite satisfied with his progress, and his ordinary salary was raised to two pounds. It was summertime, and the accumulation of his commissions justified the family moving into larger rooms, one of which was to be a bathroom. But Mr. Pinwell was beginning to feel his health very much affected, and he looked forward with intense avidity to the two weeks' holiday which was his due in September. In July he achieved a great triumph. He met and got into the good graces of the great Mr. Clappe. As Senner junior predicted, that gentleman had quite forgotten their previous meeting, and it happened in the company of the good Mr. Cherish. They all met in the bar of "The Cormorant," and after several drinks Cherish said:

"I say, Pinwell, tell Mr. Clappe that story about the sea captain!"

Mr. Pinwell complied, and when he had finished he saw the shiny bags of flesh on Mr. Clappe 's face shaking. He was evidently very much amused, although his eyes looked hard and tired. He said hoarsely:

"Damn good! What's yours?"

Mr. Pinwell did not fail on this occasion, and asked for some gin. And directly he noticed that the great man's glass was nearly empty, he insisted on ordering some more all round. He found Mr. Clappe an expensive client. He drank prodigiously, in a splendid nonchalant manner, hardly noticing it, or taking any interest in who paid for it. It took Mr. Pinwell several weeks, and cost him the price of several whole bottles of whisky, before he became sufficiently established in favor to solicit orders. But once having arrived there, the rest was easy, for Mr. Clappe had the reputation of being '4oyal to his pals," and he had the power of placing very large orders.

There came a day when Mr. Pinwell received an order for over eight hundred pounds' worth of goods, and for the first time in his life he got very drunk. He arrived home in a cab very late at night and was just conscious enough to tell his wife that he had been taken ill, and some one had given him some brandy, and it had gone to his head. She helped him to bed, and seemed rather surprised and alarmed.

On the following day he was very ill, and a doctor was sent for. He examined him carefully, and looked stern. Out in the hall he said to Mrs. Pinwell:

"Excuse me, Mrs. Pinwell, but does your husband drink rather a lot?" "Drink!" exclaimed the lady. "My Tom? ... Why, he's practically a teetotaler."

The doctor looked at her thoughtfully and murmured," Oh!" Then, as he turned to go, he said:

"Well, we'll pull him through this, I hope, but he must be very careful. You must advise him never to touch alcohol in any form. It's poison to him," and he left Mrs. Pinwell speechless with indignation. Mr. Pinwell's illness proved more obstinate than was anticipated, and it was some weeks before he was well enough to get about. When he arrived at that stage the firm of Dollbones were considerate enough to suggest that he might take his holiday earlier than had been arranged, and go away at once.

Consequently, on a certain fine morning in August, Mr. and Mrs. Pinwell, with the two children, set out for a fortnight's holiday to Heme Bay. The firm paid his salary while he was away, and in addition he had now nearly thirty-five pounds in the bank, and all his debts were paid. It was many years since the family had been in such an affluent position, and everything pointed to the prospect of a joyous and beneficial time. And so indeed, to a large extent, it was. Mr. Pinwell felt very shaky when he arrived, and he spent most of his time sitting in a deck chair on the sands, watching the children, while his wife sat on the sands by his side, sewing. The fresh breezes from the Channel made him very sleepy at first, but he gradually got used to them. It was extremely pleasant sitting there listening to the waves breaking on the shore and watching the white sails of yachts gliding hither and thither; very pleasant and very refreshing. It was only after some days that when he was left alone a certain moroseness came over him. He could not explain this to himself; it seemed so unreasonable. But he felt a curious and restless desire and an irritability. These moods became more pronounced as the week advanced, in spite of the fact that his strength returned to him. He had moods when he wished to be alone and the children tired him.

On the fifth day, he and his wife were strolling up from the beach late in the afternoon, and they were nearing their lodgings when he suddenly said:

"I think I'll just stroll round and get a paper."

"Oh! Shall I come with you?" his wife asked.

"No, no, my dear. Don't. Er-I'll just stroll round by myself-"

He seemed so anxious to go by himself that she did not insist, and he sauntered round the corner. He looked back to see that she had gone in, and then he walked rather more quickly round into the High Street. He hummed to himself and glanced rather furtively at the contents of the newspaper bills, then, after looking up and down the street, he suddenly darted into the saloon bar of the principal hotel. ...

After his second glass of gin-and-water a feeling of comfortable security crept over him. After all, it was a very ingratiating atmosphere this, ingratiating and sociable. He glanced round the bar and carried on a brief but formal conversation with a florid individual standing near him. He hesitated for a moment whether he would tell him the story about the sea captain, but on second thoughts decided to reserve it to a more intimate occasion. Besides, he must not be away long.

After that it became a habit with Mr. Pinwell for the rest of the holiday for him at some time during the day, and occasionally twice or three times during the day, to "go for a stroll round by himself." His wife never for one moment suspected the purpose of these wanderings, though she was informed that he was taking another bottle of the medicine.

When they returned to town Mr. Pinwell certainly seemed better and more eager about his work. It may be that he had the measure of his constitution more under control. He knew what was the least damaging drink he could take, and he knew how much he dare consume without immediately disastrous results. He gradually became a well-known habitue of all the best-known saloon bars in the neighborhood of his rounds. His character altered. He always remained mild and unassertive, but his face became pinched and thin, and he began to enjoy the reputation of being a "knowing one." He did not make a fortune in his solicitations for orders for gimp, trimmings, buttons, and embroidery, but he certainly earned a very fair competence. In two years' time he was entirely intimate with every buyer of importance in the Camling Town district and out as far as the "Teck Arms" at Highgate. The family still occupied the larger rooms (with the bathroom) that they had moved to, and both the girls attended the Camling Town Collegiate School for Girls, and showed every promise of being worthy and attractive members of society.

It was not till the end of the second year that two events following rapidly on each other's heels tended to disturb the normal conditions of the Pinwell family. A letter arrived one day from a lawyer.
It appeared that a brother of Mr. Pinwell's whom he had not seen for twelve years, and who had owned a farm in Northamptonshire, had died intestate. He was not married, and Tom Pinwell was his only living relative. Under the circumstances he inherited the whole of his brother's property.

When this had been assessed it was proved to be worth £140 per year. Needless to say this news brought great joy to the traveler's family. Visions of great splendor opened out before them, wealth, comfort, security. The day after the settlement was made, Tom Pinwell entertained Mr. Cherish, Mr. Clappe, and a few others of his friends to a supper at "The Queen of Roumania," and the next day he was taken Very ill. He lay in a critical state for ten days, nursed with a sort of feline intensity by his wife. The doctor then said that he might recover-he was a different doctor to the one who had so exasperated Mrs. Pinwell with his outrageous suggestions- but that he would be an invalid all his life. He would have to live on special food and must not touch either sweets or alcohol in any form.

On a certain evening Mr. Pinwell showed traces of convalescence and was allowed to sit up in bed. His wife as usual sat by his bedside, knitting. He seemed more cheerful than he had ever been before, and Mrs. Pinwell took the opportunity of saying:

"What a blessing it is, dear, about this money!"

"Yes, dear," answered her spouse.

"Do you know, Tom," she said suddenly, "there is a thing I've Wanted to do all my life. And now perhaps is the opportunity."

"What is that, my dear?"

"To go and live in the country."

"Yes, dear."

"Think of it! When you're better, we can go and get a little cottage somewhere, with a bit of a garden, you know-grow our own vegetables and that. You can live fine in some parts of the country for £140 a year. You'll be able to give up this nasty tiring old business. It'll be lovely."

"Yes, my dear."

Mr. Pinwell's voice sounded rather faint, and she busied herself with his beef tea. Nothing more was said about the idea that night. But gradually, as he got stronger, Mrs. Pinwell enlarged on the idea. She talked about the flowers they could grow, and the economy of having your own fowls and potatoes. It would have to be right in the country, but not too far from a village or town, so that the girls could continue their schooling and meet other girls. To all of this Mr. Pinwell agreed faintly, and he even made a suggestion that he thought Surrey was nicer than Buckinghamshire.

Mr. Pinwell was confined to his bedroom for nearly two months. And then one day a letter came from Messrs. Dollbones. It was to say that in view of the short time that Mr. Pinwell had been in their service they could not see their way to continue paying his salary after the end of the month, unless he were well enough to continue his work.

Mrs. Pinwell said:

"No, and they needn't continue to pay it at all, for all we care!"

A troubled look came over her husband's face, and he said:

"Um-they've treated me very well, Emma, very well indeed. There's many firms don't pay their employees at all when they're ill."

"Well then, they jolly well ought to," answered Mrs. Pinwell. "People get ill through doing the firm's work."

Mr. Pinwell sniffed. It was the one subject upon which he and his wife were inclined to differ. Mrs. Pinwell did not understand business; she had no reverence for it.

By the end of the month Mr. Pinwell was up again and going for short walks up and down the street. One day he said:

"Let me see, my dear-next Thursday is the first of the new month, isn't it?" "Yes," answered Mrs. Pinwell. "And thank goodness you haven't got to go back to that horrid old business!">

Mr. Pinwell said nothing at the time, but a few hours later he said:

"Er-I've been thinking, my dear. I rather think I ought perhaps to-er-to try and see if I could go for a little while on Thursday. You see, the firm have treated me very generously, very generously indeed-and-er-business is business"

"What does it matter?" answered his wife. "I 'm sure they've got some one else doing your job by now. Besides, you're not strong enough."

Mr. Pinwell fidgeted with his watch-chain and walked up the street. During the next two days Mrs. Pinwell could tell that he was fretting. He seemed distracted and inclined to be irritable. He gave demonstrations of his walking powers and stayed out longer and moved more quickly. He got into such a state on the Wednesday evening, that in a weak moment Mrs. Pinwell made the mistake of her life.

She agreed that he might try and go the next day just for an hour or so, but he was to come home directly he felt tired.

Tom started out on the Thursday morning, and he seemed in a great state of elation. In spite of his weakness he insisted on taking one of his bags of samples. He walked more quickly down the street than she had seen him walk for a long time. Mrs. Pinwell then turned to her household duties. She was disappointed, but not entirely surprised, that her husband did not come home to lunch, but at half-past three a sudden curious feeling of alarm came over her. She tried to reason with herself that it was all nonsense; nothing had happened, Tom was a little late-that was all. But her reason quailed before some more insidious sense of calamity. The children came home from school at a quarter-past four, and still he had not returned. She gave them their tea and somehow their gay chatter irritated her for the first time. She would not convey to them her sense of fear. She washed up the tea-things and busied herself in the house.

It was a quarter to six when Tom came home. He staggered into the hall. His eyes had a strange look she had not seen before. He was trembling violently. She did not ask any questions. She took his arm and led him into the bedroom and untied his collar and tie. He lay on the bed and his teeth chattered. She got him a hot-water bottle and gradually undressed him. Then she sent one of the girls for the doctor.

In the meantime he started talking incoherently, although he repeated on one or two occasions, "I've taken another bottle of the medicine, Emm'."

The doctor was on duty in the surgery when the child called, and he did not come round till half-past eight.

When he looked at Pinwell and took his pulse, he said: "What's he been doing?"

"He's been out," said Mrs. Pinwell. "He said he'd taken another bottle of the medicine."

"Medicine? what medicine?" The doctor seemed to examine the lips of the sick man very closely, then he shook his head. He turned to Mrs. Pinwell as though he were going to make a statement, then he changed his mind. It did not require any great astuteness to determine from the doctor's face that the case was critical. He gave the patient a powder, and after a few instructions to Mrs. Pinwell he went, and said he would return later in 'he evening. After the doctor had gone, Mr. Pinwell was delirious for an hour, and then he sank into a deep sleep. The doctor returned just after eleven. He examined him and said that nothing more could be done that night. He would return in the morning. In the meantime, if things took a more definite turn, they could send for him.

Tom Pinwell lay unconscious for nearly twenty-four hours, sometimes mumbling feverishly, at other times falling into a deep coma. But suddenly, late on the following evening, he seemed to alter. His face cleared, and he sighed peacefully. Mrs. Pinwell noticed the change and she went up close to the bed. He looked at her and said suddenly:

"I don't think it would do, my dear, to go and live in the country." "No, no, dear; all right. We'll live where you like."

"You see," he said after a pause," business has to be gone through .... There was Judkins & Cd., they treated me very fair, then they went bankrupt. It was very unfortunate, very unfortunate indeed .... I wouldn't like these people-what's their name, Emma? ... "

"Dollbones."

"Ah, yes, Dollbones! ... Dollbones. No, I wouldn't like them to think I'd let them in like. Just because I had a little money.... It's a very serious thing business ... "

Mr. Pinwell seemed about to say something, but he smiled instead and looked up at the ceiling. He became very still after that, and Mrs. Pinwell placed a book so that the candle-light should not shine on his face. All through the night she sat there watching and doing the little things the doctor had told her to. But he was very still. Once he sighed, and on another occasion she thought he said:

hot-water bottle and gradually undressed him. Then she sent one of the girls for the doctor.

In the meantime he started talking incoherently, although he repeated on one or two occasions, "I've taken another bottle of the medicine, Emm'."

The doctor was on duty in the surgery when the child called, and he did not come round till half-past eight.

When he looked at Pinwell and took his pulse, he said: "What's he been doing?"

"He's been out," said Mrs. Pinwell. "He said he'd taken another bottle of the medicine."

"Medicine? what medicine?" The doctor seemed to examine the lips of the sick man very closely, then he shook his head. He turned to Mrs. Pinwell as though he were going to make a statement, then he changed his mind. It did not require any great astuteness to determine from the doctor's face that the case was critical. He gave the patient a powder, and after a few instructions to Mrs. Pinwell he went, and said he would return later in 'he evening. After the doctor had gone, Mr. Pinwell was delirious for an hour, and then he sank into a deep sleep. The doctor returned just after eleven. He examined him and said that nothing more could be done that night. He would return in the morning. In the meantime, if things took a more definite tum, they could send for him.

Tom Pinwell lay unconscious for nearly twenty-four hours, sometimes mumbling feverishly, at other times falling into a deep coma. But suddenly, late on the following evening, he seemed to alter. His face cleared, and he sighed peacefully. Mrs. Pinwell noticed the change and she went up close to the bed. He looked at her and said suddenly:

"I don't think it would do, my dear, to go and live in the country." "No, no, dear; all right. We'll live where you like."

"You see," he said after a pause," business has to be gone through .... There was Judkins & Cd., they treated me very fair, then they went bankrupt. It was very unfortunate, very unfortunate indeed .... I wouldn't like these people-what's their name, Emma? ... "

"Dollbones."

"Ah, yes, Dollbones! ... Dollbones. No, I wouldn't like them to think I'd let them in like. Just because I had a little money.... It's a very serious thing business ... "

Mr. Pinwell seemed about to say something, but he smiled instead and looked up at the ceiling. He became very still after that, and Mrs. Pinwell placed a book so that the candle-light should not shine on his face. All through the night she sat there watching and doing the little things the doctor had told her to. But he was very still. Once he sighed, and on another occasion she thought he said:

"That was very amusin' about that invoice of Barrel and Beelswright, Mr. Cherish . . . oh, dear me!"

About dawn, thoroughly exhausted with her vigil, Mrs. Pinwell fell into a fitful sleep, sitting up in her chair. She only slept for a few minutes, and then awakened with a start. The short end of candle was spluttering in its socket, and its light was contending with the cold blue glimmer of the early day. She shivered, her frame racked by physical fatigue, and her mind benumbed by the incredible stillness of the little room.

"Consequently, ladies and gentlemen, after placing £17,500 in the reserve fund, for the reasons which I have indicated to you, I feel justified in recommending a dividend of 12 per cent, on the ordinary shares."

The big man with the square chin dabbed his forehead with his handkerchief and took a sip of water as he resumed his seat. A faint murmur of approval and applause ran round the room; papers rustled, and people spoke in low, breathless voices. Twelve and a half per cent! It was a good dividend, a very good dividend! A hundred different brains visualized rapidly what it meant to them personally. To some it meant a few extra luxuries, to others comforts, and to some a distinct social advance. If Dollbones could only keep this up!

Sir Arthur Schelling was seconding the adoption of this report, but it was a mere formality. No one took any interest in the white-haired financier, except to nudge each other and say, "That's Schelling. They say he's worth half a million." It was a curiously placid meeting, there was no criticism, and every one seemed on the best of terms. It broke up, and the shareholders dispersed into little knots, or scattered to spread the good news that Dollbones were paying twelve and a half per cent.

Sir Arthur took the chairman's hand and murmured:

"I must congratulate you, Hylam. An excellent report!"

The large man almost blushed with pleasure, and said:

"It's very kind of you, Sir Arthur. Are you lunching in town?"

"I was going to suggest that you lunch with me at the Carlton. I have my car here."

"Oh! thank you very much. I shall be delighted."

Mr. Hylam turned and gave a few instructions to his lawyer and his private secretary, and handed various papers to each; then he followed his host out of the Cannon Street Hotel.

They got into the great car, and each man lighted a well-merited cigar. As they drove through the city, Sir Arthur discussed a few details of the balance-sheet, and then added:

"I really think you have shown a remarkable genius of organization in conducting this business, Hylam. It is a business which I should imagine requires considerable technical knowledge and great—er—tact."

Mr. Hylam laughed deprecatingly and muttered:

"Oh, we have our little difficulties!" He puffed at his cigar and looked out of the window.

"So many—er—varieties of employees, I should imagine?" said Sir Arthur.

"Yes, you're right, sir. There are varieties. I've had a lot of difficulty with the travelers this year." He gave a vicious puff at his cigar and stamped on the ash on the floor, and suddenly exclaimed:

"Drunken swine!"

Sir Arthur readjusted his gold-rimmed pince-nez and looked at his friend.

"Is that so indeed?"

"Yes," answered Mr. Hylam. "I don't know how it is. They nearly all drink. In one district alone, I've had two travelers practically drink themselves to death, one after the other."

"I'm very distressed to hear that," said Sir Arthur; "very distressed. It's a very great social evil. My wife, as you may know, is on a board of directorship of the Blue Bib and Evangelists. They do a lot of good work. They have a branch in Camling Town. They have pleasant evenings, you know—cocoa and bagatelle, and so on; and lectures on Sunday. But, I don't know, it doesn't seem to eradicate the evil."

"No; I'm afraid it's in the blood with many of them," said the managing director.

"Yes, that's very true. I often tell my wife I'm afraid she wastes her time. It seems inexplicable. I can't see why they should do it. What satisfaction can it be to—er—drink to excess? And then it must hamper them so in the prosecution of their work. It seems in a way so—ungrateful, to the people who employ them, I mean. Ah! here we are at the Carlton! Champneys, come back for me at—er—three thirty. Yes, it's a great social evil, a very great social evil indeed!"

## George

There was something essentially Chinese about the appearance of George as he lay there propped up against the pillows. His large, flabby face had an expression of complete detachment. His narrowing eyes regarded me with a fatalistic repose. Observing him I felt that nothing mattered, nothing ever had mattered, and nothing ever would matter. And I was angry. Pale sunlight filtered through the curtains.

'Good Lord!' I exclaimed. 'Still in bed! Do you know it's nearly twelve o'clock?'

An almost inaudible sigh greeted my explosion. George occupied the maisonnette below me. Some fool of an uncle had left him a small private income, and he lived alone, attended by an old housekeeper. He did nothing, absolutely nothing at all, not even amuse himself; and whenever I went in to see him he was invariably in bed. There was nothing wrong with his health. It was sheer laziness. But not laziness of a negative kind, mark you, but the outcome of a calm and studied policy. I knew this, and it angered me the more.

'What would happen if the whole world went on like you?' I snapped.

He sighed again, and then replied in his thin, mellow voice:—

'We should have a series of ideal states. There would be no wars, no crimes, no divorce, no competition, no greed, envy, hatred, or malice.'

'Yes, and no food.'

He turned slightly on one side. His accents became mildly expostulating—the philosopher fretted by an ignorant child.

'How unreasonable you are, dear boy. How unthinking! The secret of life is complete immobility. The tortoise lives four hundred years; the fox terrier wears itself out in ten. Wild beasts, fishes, savages, and stockbrokers fight and struggle and eat each other up. The only place for a cultivated man is bed. In bed he is supreme—the arbiter of his sold. His limbs and the vulgar carcass of his being constructed for purely material functioning are concealed. His head rules him. He is the autocrat of the bolster, the gallant of fine linen, the master of complete relaxation. Believe me, there are a thousand tender attitudes of repose unknown to people like you. The four corners of a feather bed are an inexhaustible field of luxurious adventure. I have spent more than half my life in bed, and even now I have not explored all the delectable crannies and comforts that it holds for me.'

'No,' I sneered. 'And in the meantime, other people have to work to keep you there.'

'That is not my fault. A well-ordered state should be a vast caravansary of dormitories. Ninety-nine per cent of these activities you laud so extravagantly are gross and unnecessary. People should be made to stay in bed till they have found out something worth doing. Who wants telephones, and cinemas, and safety razors? All that civilization has invented are vulgar luxuries and time-saving devices. And when they have saved the time they don't know what to do with it. All that is required is bread, and wine, and fine linen. I, even I, would not object to getting up for a few hours every week to help to produce these things.'

He stroked the three weeks' growth on his chin, and smiled magnanimously. Then he continued: 'The world has yet to appreciate the real value of passivity. In a crude form the working classes have begun to scratch the edge of the surface. They have discovered the strike. Now, observe that the strike is the most powerful political weapon of the present day. It can accomplish nearly everything it requires, and yet it is a condition of immobility. So you see already that immobility may be more powerful that activity. But this is only the beginning. When the nations start going to bed and stopping there, then civilization will take a leap forward. You can do nothing with a man in bed — not even knock him down. My ambition is to form a league of bedfellows. So that if one day some busybody or group of busybodies says.

"We're going to war with France, or Germany, or America," we can reply, "Very well. Then I'm going to bed." Then, after a time, they would have to go to bed too. And they would eventually succumb to the gentle caresses of these sheets and eiderdowns. All their evil intentions would melt away. The world should be ruled, not by Governments or Soviets, but by national doss-houses.'

He yawned, and I pulled up the blind.

'What about the good activities?' I replied.

For a second I thought I had stumped him, or that he was not going to deign to reply. Then the thin rumble of his voice reached me from across the sheets:—

'What you call the good activities can all be performed in bed. That is to say, they can be substituted by a good immobility. The activities of man are essentially predatory. He has learned nothing and forgotten nothing. He is a hunter and slayer, and nothing else at all. All his activities are diversions of this instinct. Commerce is war, capital is a sword, labor is a stomach. Progress means either filling the stomach, or chopping someone else's head off with the sword. Science is an instrument that speeds up the execution. Politics is a game of fan-tan. Colonization is straightforward daylight robbery.'

'I'm not going to waste my morning with a fool,' I- said. 'But what about art, and beauty, and charity, and love?'

'In bed,' he mumbled. 'All in bed. They are all of them spiritual things. Bed is the place for them. Was Keats 's "Ode to a Nightingale" any finer because he got up and wrote it down, and sent it to a fool of a publisher? Charity! Give a man a bed, and charity ceases to have any significance. You have given him a kingdom. There he may weave beauty and romance. Love! What a fool you are! Is a bed a less suitable place for love than a County Council tramcar?'

His voice died away above the coverlet. I was about to deliver a vitriolic tirade against his ridiculous theories, but I did not know where to begin, and before I had framed a suitable opening the sound of gentle snoring reached me.

I record this conversation as faithfully as I can recollect, because it will help you to share with me the sense of extreme surprise at certain events which followed, two months later. Of course, George did occasionally get up. Sometimes he went for a gentle stroll in the afternoon, and he belonged to a club downtown where he would go and dine in the evening. After dinner he would watch some of the men play billiards, but he invariably returned to his bed about ten o'clock. He never played any game himself; neither did he, apparently, write or receive letters. Occasionally he read in bed, but he never looked at a newspaper or a magazine. He once said to me that if you read the newspapers you might as well play golf; and the tremulous shiver of disgust in his voice when he uttered the word 'golf' is a thing I shall never forget.

I ask you, then, to imagine my amazement when, two months later, George shaved himself, got up to breakfast, reached a City office at nine o'clock, worked all day, and returned at seven in the evening. You will no doubt have a shrewd idea of the reason, and you are right. She was the prettiest little thing you can imagine, with chestnut hair, and a solemn babyish pucker of the lips. She was as vital as he was turgid. Her name was Maisie Brand. I don't know how he met her, but Maisie, in addition to being pretty and in every way attractive, was a practical modern child. George's two hundred a year might be sufficient to keep him in bed, but it wasn't going to be enough to run a household on. Maisie had no use for this bed theory. She was a daughter of sunshine and fresh air, and frocks and theatres, and social life. If George was to win her he must get up in the morning.

On the Sunday after the dramatic change I visited him in his bedroom. He was like a broken man. He groaned when he recognized me.

'I suppose you'll stop in bed all day to-day?' I remarked jauntily.

''I've got to get up this afternoon,' he growled. 'I've got to take her to a concert.'

'Well, how do you like work?' I asked.

'It's torture. Agony. It's awful. Fortunately, I found a fellow sufferer. He works next to me. We take it in turns to have twenty-minute naps, while the other keeps watch.'

I laughed, and quoted: 'Custom lies upon us with a weight, heavy as frost and deep almost as night.' Then I added venomously:—

'Well, I haven't any sympathy for you. It serves you right for the way you've gone on all these years.'

I thought he was asleep again, but at last his drowsy accents proclaimed:—

'What a perfect fool you are! You always follow the line of least resistance.'

I laughed outright at that, and exclaimed, 'Well, if ever there was a case of the pot calling the kettle black!'

There was a long interval, during Which I seemed to observe a slow, cumbrous movement in the bed. Doubtless he was exploring. When he spoke again there was a faint tinge of animation in his voice:—

'You are not capable, I suppose, of realizing the danger of it all. You fool!

Do you think I follow the line of least resistance in bed? Do you think I haven't often wanted to get up and do all these ridiculous things you and your kind indulge in? Can't you see what might happen? Suppose these dormant temptations were thoroughly aroused! My heavens! It's awful to contemplate. Habit, you say? Yes, I know. I know quite well the risk I am running. Am I to sacrifice all the epic romance of this life between the sheets for the sordid round of petty actions you call life? I was a fool to get up that day. I had a premonition of danger when I awoke at dawn. I said to myself, "George, restrain yourself. Do not be deceived by the hollow sunlight. Above all things, keep clear of the park." But, like a fool, I betrayed my sacred trust. The premonitions which come to one in bed are always right. I got up. And now — By jove! It's too late!'

Smothered sobs seemed to shake the bed.

'Well,' I said, 'if you feel like that about it, if you think more of your bed than of the girl, I should break it off. She won't be missing much.'

He suddenly sat up and exclaimed:

'Don't you dare—'

Then he sank back on the pillow, and added dispassionately:—

'There, you see already the instinct of activity. A weak attitude. I could crush you more successfully with complete immobility. But these movements are already beginning. They shake me at every turn. Nothing is secure.'

Inwardly chuckling at his discomfiture, I left him.

During the months that followed I did not have opportunities of studying George to the extent that I should have liked, as my work carried me to various parts of the country; but what opportunities I did have I found sufficiently interesting. He certainly improved in health. A slight color tinged his cheeks. He seemed less puffy and turgid. His movements were still slow, but they were more deliberate than of old. His clothes were neat and brushed. The girl was delightful. She came up and chatted with! me, and we became great friends. She talked to me quite frankly about George. She laughed about his passion for bed, but declared she meant to knock all that sort of thing out of him. She was going to wake him up thoroughly. She said laughingly that she thought it was perfectly disgusting the way he had been living. I used to try to visualize George making love to her, but somehow the picture would never seem convincing. I do not think it could have been a very passionate affair. Passion was the last thing you would associate with George. I used to watch them walking down the street, the girl slim and vivid, swinging along with broad strides; George, rather flustered and disturbed, pottering along by her side; like a performing bear that is being led away from its bun. He did not appear to look at her, and when she addressed him vivaciously he bent forward his head and held his large ear close to. her face. It was as though he were timid of her vitality.

At first the spectacle amused me, but after a time it produced in me another feeling.

'This girl is being thrown away on him. It's horrible. She's much too good for George.' And when I was away I was constantly thinking of her, and dreading the day of the wedding, praying that something would happen to prevent it. But, to my deep concern, nothing did happen to prevent it, and they were duly married in April.

They went for a short honeymoon to Brittany, and then returned and occupied George's old maisonnette below me. The day after their return I had to face a disturbing realization. I was falling hopelessly in love with Maisie myself. I could not think of George, or take any interest in him. I was always thinking of her. Her face haunted me. Her charm and beauty, and the pathos of her position, gripped me. I made up my mind that the only thing to do was to go away. I went to Scotland, and on my return took a small flat in another part of London. I wrote to George and gave him my address, and wished him all possible luck. I said I hoped 'some day' to pay them a visit, but if at any time I could be of service would he let me know?

I cannot describe to you the anguish I experienced during the following twelve months. I saw nothing of George or Maisie at all, but the girl was ever present in my thoughts. I could not work. I lived in a state of feverish restlessness. Time and again I was on the point of breaking my resolve, but I managed to keep myself in hand.

It was in the following June that I met Maisie herself, walking down Regent Street. She looked pale and worried. Dark rings encircled her eyes. She gave a little gasp when she saw me, and clutched my hand. I tried to be formal, but she was obviously laboring under some tense emotion.

'My flat is in Baker Street,' I said. 'Will you come and visit me?'

She answered huskily, 'Yes, I will come to-morrow afternoon. Thank you.'

She slipped away in the crowd. I spent a sleepless night. What had happened? Of course, I could see it all. George had gone back to bed. Having once secured her, his efforts had gradually flagged. He had probably left his business—or been sacked—and spent the day sleeping. The poor girl was probably living a life of loneliness

and utter poverty. What was I to do? All day long I paced up and down my flat. I dread ed that she might not com e. It was just after four that the bell rang. I hastened to answer it myself. It was she. I led her into the sitting-room and tried to be formal and casual. I made some tea and chatted impersonally about the weather and the news of the day. She hardly answered me. Suddenly she buried her face in her hands and broke into tears. I sprang to her and patted her shoulder.

'There, there!' I said. 'What is it? Tell me all about it, Maisie.'

'I can't live with him. I can't live with him any longer,' she sobbed.

I must acknowledge that my heart gave a violent bump, not entirely occasioned by contrition. I murmured as sympathetically as I could, but with prophetic assurance:—

'He's gone back to bed?'

'Oh, no,' she managed to stammer. 'It's not that. It's just the opposite.' 'Just the opposite!'

'He's so restless, so exhausting. Oh, dear! Yes, please, Mr. Wargrave, give me a' cup of tea, and I will tell you all about it.'

For a moment I wondered whether the poor girl 's mental balance had been upset. I poured her out the tea in silence. George restless! George exhausting! Whatever did she mean? She sipped the tea meditatively; then she dabbed her beautiful eyes and told me the following remarkable story.

'It was all right at first, Mr. Wargrave. We were quite happy. He was still—you know, very lazy, very sleepy. It all came about gradually. Every week, however, he seemed to get a little more active and vital. He began to sleep shorter hours and work longer. He liked to be entertained in the evening or to go to a theatre. On Sundays he would go for quite long walks. It went on like that for months. Then they raised his position in the firm. He seemed to open out. It was as though during all those years he had spent in bed he had been hoarding up remarkable stores of energy. And suddenly some demon of restlessness got possession of him. He began to work frenziedly. At first he was pleasant to me; then he became so busy he completely ignored me. At the end of six months they made him manager of a big engineering works at Waltham Green. One of the directors, a Mr. Sturge, said to me one day, "This husband of yours is a remarkable man. He is the most forceful person we have ever employed. What has he been doing all these years? Why haven't we heard of him before?" He would get up at six in the morning, have a cold bath, and study for two hours before he went off to work. He would work all day like a fury. They say he was a perfect slave-driver in the works. Only last week he sacked a man for taking a nap five minutes over his lunch hour. He would get home about eight o'clock, have a hurried dinner, and then insist on going to the opera or playing bridge. When we got back he would read till two or three in the morning. Oh, Mr. Wargrave, he has got worse and worse. He never sleeps at all. He terrifies me. On Sunday it is just the same. He works all the morning. After lunch he motors out to North wood and plays eighteen holes before tea and eighteen after.'

'What!' I exclaimed. 'Golf!'

'Golf, and science, and organization are his manias. They say he's invented some wonderful labor-saving appliances on the plant, and he's planning all kinds of future activities. The business of the firm is increasing enormously. They pay him well, but he still persists in living in that maisonnette. He says he's too busy to move.'

'Is he cruel to you?'

'If complete indifference and neglect is cruelty, he is most certainly cruel. Sometimes he gives me a most curious look, as though he hated me and yet he can't account for me! He allows me no intimacy of any sort. If I plead with him he does n 't answer. I believe he holds me responsible for all these dormant powers which have got loose and which he cannot now control. I do not think his work gives him any satisfaction. It is as though he were driven on by some blind force. Oh, Mr. Wargrave, I can't go on. It is killing me. I must run away and leave him.'

'Maisie,' I murmured, and I took her hand.

The immediate subsequent proceedings are not perhaps entirely necessary to record in relating this story, which is essentially George's story. The story of Maisie and myself could comfortably fill a stout volume, but as it concerns two quite unremarkable people, who were just human and workaday, I do not expect that you would be interested to read it. In any case, we have no intention of writing it, so do not be alarmed.

I can only tell you that during that year of her surprising married life Maisie had thought of me not a little, and this denouement rapidly brought things to a head. After this confession we used to meet every day. We went for rambles, and picnics, and to matinees; and, of course, that kind of thing cannot go on indefinitely. We both detested the idea of an intrigue. And eventually we decided that we would cut the Gordian knot and make a full confession. Maisie left him and went to live with a married sister.

That same morning I called on George. I arrived at the maisonnette just before six o'clock, as I knew that that was the most likely time to catch him. Without any preliminary ceremony I made my way into the familiar bedroom. George was in bed. I stood by the door and called out to him loudly: 'George!'

Like a flash he was out of bed and standing in his pyjamas; facing me. He had changed considerably. His face was lined and old, but his eyes blazed with a fury of activity. He awed me. I stammered out my confession.

'George, I 'm awfully sorry, old chap. I have a confession to make to you. It comes in the first place from Maisie. She has decided that she cannot live with you any longer. She thinks you have neglected her and treated her badly. She refuses to come back to you under any circumstances. Indeed, she—she and I—er—'

I tailed off dismally, and looked at him. For a moment I thought he was going to bear down on me. I know that if he had I should have been supine. I should have stood there and let him slaughter me. I felt completely overpowered by the force of his personality. I believe I shivered. He hovered by the edge of the bed, then he turned and looked out of the window. He stood there solemnly for nearly a minute, then he emitted a profound sigh. Without more ado he got back into bed. There was an immense upheaval of the sheets. He seemed to be burrowing down into some vast and as yet unexplored cave of comfort. He rolled and heaved, and at length became inert. I stood there, waiting for my answer. Sparrows twittered outside on the window box. I don 't know how long I waited. I felt that I could not go until he had spoken.

At length his voice came. It seemed to reach me across dim centuries of memory, an old, tired, cosy, enormously contented, sleep-encrusted voice:—

'S 'll right,' said the voice. 'Tell Mrs. Chase she needn't bring up my shaving water this morning.'

The Baby Grand

*THE STRANGE WAY IN WHICH A PIANO AFFECTED THE DESTINIES OF THE GABRIL FAMILY*

I

When the Gabril family first came to live in Camden Town, Gabril was not their name. They were reputed to have come from the Polish borderland of Prussia, and to have arrived with a name that was quite beyond the neighborhood's ability to pronounce. Some local genius invented the name of Gabril for them, that being probably an abbreviation of their original and more grandiose patronymic.

They were of Jewish stock, but had long ceased to practice or conform to any religious creed. It may almost be said that they had ceased to conform to any ethical creed. They were a thoroughly unpleasant family.

Solomon Gabril, the father, was a piano tuner. He had been married twice, and both his wives had died. By his first wife he had two sons and two daughters, Paul, Mischa, Selma, and Katie; by his second wife one daughter, Lena.

At the time when this story commences, Paul and Mischa were in the early twenties, Selma was eighteen, Katie seventeen, and Lena thirteen. They lived in three rooms and a scullery in a dingy house in Benthall Street.

Solomon was a thoroughly competent piano tuner, otherwise it is quite certain that a prominent firm of piano manufacturers in Kentish Town would not have tolerated him. He was dirty, untidy, wheezy, and vacillating. He indulged in drinking bouts, when nothing would be seen of him for days. When sober, his manner was ingratiating and somewhat facetious. He had a perpetual sneering grin.

He was, however, not entirely without feeling, and not entirely a fool. He was not capable of studied cruelty. He wished well toward his family, and would have given them the best of everything if it hadn't been that there was barely enough for his own indulgences, and self came first. He paid the rent, allowed Selma, the eldest girl, a sufficient weekly sum to buy the bare necessities of life for the rest, and he never struck the children.

It cannot be said that either of his sons had so good a character. Paul was frankly what is known as a "bad egg." He had twice been sent to prison for petty thefts. He never kept a situation for more than a few weeks. He was idle, depraved, and quarrelsome.

Mischa was less objectionable than his brother. He was quieter and had never been convicted of crime, but he was phlegmatic, morose, and stupid. He worked in a candle factory.

Selma was a narrow strip of a girl, with eyes too close together. She surreptitiously withheld money meant for the food of the family and spent it on trinkets. She was furtive and selfish. She was supposed to manage the household and to do the cooking and cleaning; and during such time as she could spare from the local picture house, she did make some sort of effort in this direction.

Katie, who did various odd jobs in tea shops and private houses, was more like her brother Mischa. She was of the flaccid kind, and sighed her way through the dreary monotony of her days.

The whole family lived in a continuous state of hunger and irritation, with the exception of Mr. Gabril. He was not particularly interested in eating, but he managed to get a good dinner every day at a coffee shop, and drank sufficient beer both to satisfy himself and to keep in a static condition of oleaginous indifference to the troubles of others.

Being, as it were, grafted upon this deplorable family tree, one may readily imagine that the conditions and prospects of the youngest child, Lena, were anything but roseate. She was obviously different from the rest. Her mother, who had been a singer, died at Lena's birth. The child had a broad, plump face and dark brown, reflective eyes. She was curiously reserved. She endured the insults and bullying of her sisters and the cuffs of her elder brother with almost uncanny fortitude, as if, when all was said and done, she was stronger than they, as if she had enduring treasures to defend.

She was sent to the local board school, more with the idea of getting her out of the way and keeping her out of mischief than of benefiting her by means of the education obtainable at that institution. Having bundled her off to school, the family's interest in her education and progress vanished; but it was instilled into her in early life that she was the only one who contributed nothing to the general upkeep of the house, and that the sooner she grew up and went out and earned her living the better it would be for her.

She slept in one bedroom with her two stepsisters, the three men occupied the other, and the third room was facetiously dubbed "the parlor" by Mr. Gabril. It was the room where the whole family congregated, fed, quarreled, and indulged in whatever recreations were available. It was furnished with a dilapidated sofa, four cane chairs, two packing cases used as chairs, a deal table, a fitted cupboard, an oleograph of King Edward as an admiral, and several colored plates taken from Christmas numbers. It had a smell of its own, in which fish, cabbage, smoke, drying clothes, and unwashed humanity mingled in degrees varying with the time of day and the state of the weather.

Lena was not allowed to sit on the sofa, which was usually occupied by the males, or, in their absence, by the other two girls. She usually sat on an empty packing case by the window, and there she would pore over her school books, trying to learn her lessons, amid the general din, bickering, and disorder.

The family took no interest in her activities, other than those which affected themselves. On her part, she formed outside friendships and developed ambitions which she never imparted to the rest.

And then one day a most unexpected thing happened.

II

It was evening, and the family had just finished supper. The boys had gone out. Mr. Gabril was sprawling on the sofa, smoking and reading the Evening News. Selma was washing up in the scullery, Katie was making herself a blouse, and Lena was sitting on her packing case, reading, when there came a knock at the door.

"Come in!" said Mr. Gabril, and there entered a young and rather good-looking clergyman.

The surprise and the consternation of the family were immense. The visit of a policeman could not have created a greater shock. Mr. Gabril started as if he expected to be accused of some deadly vice. Katie dropped her sewing. Selma, catching sight of the visitor through the open door, swiftly wiped her hands on a dry rag and prepared to re-enter the room. Lena alone seemed unmoved.

"Mr. Gabril, I believe?" the stranger cheerily inquired.

"That's my name," replied Mr. Gabril suspiciously.

"Good evening, Mr. Gabril. I am Winscombe, of the—er—church schools. I wanted to have a word with you about your daughter. Ah, good evening, Lena!"

The mystery deepened. He nodded familiarly to Lena, who was understood to mumble some response of recognition.

Now what was this all about? The family had no particular use for clergymen, a cold, repressive, prying lot. At the same time the visitor was certainly a pleasant, gentlemanly fellow. There might be something to be got out of him. The grin returned to Mr. Gabril's face.

"Oh!" he said. "I didn't know. What's it about?"

Selma, who had entered the room, and who liked the appearance of the young man, qua young man, had a brain wave.

"Won't you sit down, sir?" she said.

"Thank you, thank you," he replied, bowing. "Your other daughters, I presume? Good evening! Good evening!"

The young clergyman sat down, and balanced his hat on his knee. Then he began speaking eagerly.

"Do you know, Mr. Gabril, we think your daughter has talent—decided talent. I expect you know she was introduced to my sister by Miss Watson, at the school, who suspected her of being musical. My sister has been giving her lessons for the last year, and she is very much impressed—very much impressed indeed. My sister is not a great musician herself, and she is of opinion that Lena should go to some one more advanced."

"Well, the deuce! The nasty, furtive little cat! Why has she said nothing about this?" reflected Mr. Gabril. Outwardly he continued to grin, and he spluttered out: "Eh? Oh, yes! Well, well!"

His mind became active. Plays the piano, eh? Well, what did the fellow want? Did he think that he, Solomon Gabril, was going to spend money on piano lessons? Was he such a fool as that?

On the other hand, if Lena could play, perhaps there was money in it. Perhaps she could go on and play at the pictures. He'd heard of girls getting two or three pounds a week at the game.

The young fellow continued to talk.

"It has all fallen out rather fortunately, I hope you'll agree. A friend of ours, a comparatively wealthy man, who is a musical patron, introduced her to Soltz, the well known professor. Lena played to him yesterday, and he, too, was impressed by her extreme promise. My friend is willing to pay for a course of lessons for her with Herr Soltz. I presume you would have no objection?"

Something for nothing was entirely in keeping with Mr. Gabril's sense of social morality; but what about this? In what way did he benefit? It wanted thinking over.

These people evidently had money. It would be much better if they gave the money to him, and he supervised the girl's musical education. On the other hand, if they taught her to play properly—well, there might be money in that. Perhaps it would be better to agree in the meantime.

"Oh, really?" he said. "Very nice, Pm sure—very nice!"

"She will of course be leaving school shortly," continued the clergyman. "Then, if she is allowed to devote her whole time to music, we think she may go far—very far indeed."

"Playing for the pictures?" said Mr. Gabril tentatively.

"Oh, further than that, I trust."

"Playing at concerts and so on?"

"Why, yes, and giving her own recitals,

and being engaged by orchestral societies, and becoming a great artist."

Mr. Gabril's eyes narrowed. He was a piano tuner. He knew something about the profession. There were people like Paderewski and Pachmann making a lot of money. It had not occurred to him to associate his scrubby little daughter with the dazzling side of a musical career. He had not known till that moment that she knew a note of music. This was a historical day in the history of the Gabril family; but it had its reaction.

III

When the clergyman had gone, Selma flared up. She was jealous and furious. She went up to Lena and said:

"You little sneak!" she said, and slapped her sister's face.

Then Mr. Gabril saw red. He grabbed Selma and screamed at her:

"You fool! Leave her alone, or I'll shake the life out of you!"

Selma cried. Lena cried. Katie joined in the general uproar, and eventually said that she felt sick and was going to bed.

Their individual emotions were at cross purposes. Selma couldn't see that her father was primarily concerned with the commercial potentialities of the situation. She accused him of taking Lena's side against her, who did all the work. She was only a drudge. She wasn't given piano lessons. Rich people didn't come chasing after her, A nice thing it was! She supposed Lena would be having dancing lessons next, and be going to Buckingham Palace to be presented at court. Selma was partially hysterical, her mind being a little confused by a film she had seen that afternoon, called "The Heir to Millions."

It was a thoroughly unpleasant evening and was not improved by the late advent of the two brothers, both rather drunk. They were too drunk to be impressed by the news about the clergyman's visit. Paul laughed boisterously.

"A parson, eh?" he kept on repeating. "Fancy a parson coming 'ere!"

He seemed to think it was quite the funniest thing that had ever happened.

For several weeks Lena was subjected to a running fire of jeering comments, vindictive on the part of her stepsisters, ironic and inane on the part of the brothers. It was only Mr. Gabril himself who displayed any kind of tolerance. He cannot be said to have shown any great sympathy, but he licked his lips, and leered, and bade the others shut up. He told romantic stories of vast fortunes made out of playing the piano.

None of the others believed him. It was a dream so outside their normal conception of life as lived in Camden Town that they could not visualize it. It was possible that romantic figures in other settings did such things, but scrubby little Lena, with whose superfluous person they had been so closely herded day and night all her wretched life—nonsense!

One day, three weeks after the clergyman's visit, a note of reality was struck. A piano arrived. It was what is known as a baby grand, and it was put in the parlor. Now this was a concrete and astonishing occurrence. A piano cost money. Amid the packing cases and flimsy furniture of the Gabrils parlor it struck a flamboyant, an alarming note. If it had been an ordinary upright piano it would not have seemed so much out of place, but a grand! Even Paul was slightly awed, and Selma disagreeably impressed.

It seemed to take up all the room, to be insolently assertive. Its contempt for the flimsy furniture oozed from its shiny black sides. It was like a large Persian cat of ancient pedigree finding itself in a room full of scraggy, ill born kittens.

Mr. Gabril chuckled with satisfaction. He ran his fingers over the keys, playing the few florid harmonies he was accustomed to indulge in on his tuning rounds. It was a fine piano.

The angle of the family's attitude toward Lena shifted a little. What if there were something in it, after all? Each one naturally thought first of his or her own interests.

"Suppose she does make money, where do I come in?"

They stood round the piano in a group and made her play. They seemed to expect some astounding miracle to happen right away. They wanted her to give some definite proof that gold would quickly flow as a result of her exertions.

They were disappointed. Lena certainly seemed to play all right, but she played very dull pieces. There was nothing about the performance to dazzle or surprise.

Nevertheless, they granted her a certain amount of freedom. She was allowed to

practice for several weeks unmolested, until the novelty of the situation began to wear off. Then they got tired of her scales, arpeggios, and repetitions. Besides, nothing was being said about paying her large sums for playing in public. Paul wouldn't let her play at all when he was in the house. Mischa brought home a young man friend who banged out jazz tunes for two evenings running. Selma began to find the piano useful for piling up plates and pans and pots.

In three months' time the baby grand had ceased to be an object of awe. Respect for it vanished. It became part and parcel of the room. Its lid was scratched and marked. It was piled up with papers and crockery and odd rubbish. Lena practiced only when the others were out, and then she was always being interrupted by knocks at the door, barrel organs in the street below, or the irksome duty of having to keep one eye on a boiling pot.

Twice a week she went over to Kensington and had a lesson from Mr. Soltz. As her father refused to give her any money, she had to walk there and back, always hungry, frequently exhausted, ill shod, shabbily dressed, rain-soaked; but her eyes continued to glow with the fire of her fixed purpose.

IV

A whole year passed before the most deplorable incident in connection with the piano happened.

Lena had left school. She was over fifteen. It was forcibly pointed out to Mr. Gabril by the other members of the family that she might now be out earning money. There was no sign yet that all this piano playing was going to be any good. She might go on doing it for years, and who was going to keep her? Why should she be allowed to idle about at home, strumming on a piano, when Katie had to go off every morning to a tea shop?

Paul was out of a job, and Selma had become engaged to a flashy young man who served in a store and backed horses. She wanted to get married, but of course they had no money to start housekeeping. That fact was probably the basis of the idea which led to the regrettable incident—that and Paul's unemployment and depravity. It is certain that at the height of this condition of discontent and disorder Paul and Selma put their heads together. They were desperate and without moral bias. They plotted a devilish dishonesty.

One day, when every one was out except these two, a gentleman in a bowler hat paid them a visit. He made a careful examination of the piano, and the three of them whispered together in a corner.

On the following Thursday afternoon Lena was over at Kensington having a lesson, Mr. Gabril was out tuning, and Katie, of course, was also at business. A van drove up. Four men in green aprons came upstairs. They picked up the baby grand as if it really was a baby. They carried it gently downstairs and deposited it in the van. The foreman handed Paul an envelope, and they drove off. Paul and Selma had sold the piano for seventy pounds!

The plot was ingenious, but somewhat incomplete. They had taken the precaution to deal with a firm in South London, and payment was made in cash. It was obvious that they must not disappear. They must brazen the thing out. Selma was to say that she was alone in the house when the piano men called and said they had instructions to take the piano away for repairs. She knew nothing about it. She supposed it was all right.

Nevertheless, it was a risky game. It all depended upon what attitude Mr. Winscombe's people might take. They might advertise. Paul and Selma would have to stick together and lie like anything. They shared the spoil, but both felt dreadfully frightened.

Curiously enough, Selma felt less afraid of detection that she did of Lena. What would Lena do? There was something queer and uncanny about the kid. You never knew what she would do.

It was unfortunate for Paul that the transaction was a cash one. He went out into the street with thirty-five pounds in his pocket. He was not a good subject to have so much money on him. He had never had so much before in his life. He was frightened and very desperate. He went straight down the road and had three whiskies.

Then he began to see things more clearly. There would be a row. He might be arrested, put in prison—anything. What did he care about the family? Thirty-five pounds seemed an enormous sum. He could live for months, and then perhaps something else might turn up—another scoop. He wasn't going back to that house.

Of course, he had promised to stick by Selma, but what did it matter? Selma could look after herself. Women were always all right. Let's have a good night out first, anyway!

Six days later Paul died in a hospital, from heart failure following an acute attack of delirium tremens. There was no money on him, and nothing to identify him. He was buried in a pauper's grave. His half share of the piano had killed him.

And Selma's? She was pluckier than Paul, and a little more cunning. To her surprise, Lena took the news more philosophically than she had expected. At first, of course, she believed Selma's story. That they had sent for the piano to do something to it; but even when the truth came out, and she knew that it had been stolen, she only seemed a little dazed and surprised. It was as if there were within her vibrant forces that could not be deflected by the mere removal of material things.

It was Mr. Gabril who caused Selma most trouble. He was furious. He saw at once that some trick had been played, and he regarded the playing of tricks as his own prerogative. For some time, indeed, he had mentally nurtured this identical idea of selling the piano, and he would have done it more efficiently. He had many friends in the piano-dealing world—friends who were capable of keeping their mouths shut, too. He would have got a good price. He did not believe there was anything in Lena's future, or, if there were, he thought it would take too long to materialize.

When Paul failed to return, the father's suspicions naturally centered upon him. He accepted Selma's statement unquestioningly. Well, what were they going to do? Selma hinted at keeping the matter quiet.

"The piano was only lent. They will hold us responsible," she said.

"Idiot!" yelled the father. "What's the good of that? They're bound to find out in time. Besides, I'm going to find out who did this dirty trick. I'm going to have my revenge!"

"Suppose it was Paul," said Selma, turning rather pale.

"If it was Paul, he can go to jail for it. He's been there before. It's about the only place he's fit for," said the boy's father.

Selma cursed her brother in her heart. The coward! The sneak! Fancy running away, leaving her to bear the brunt of the whole danger! How like a man!

Lena was chiefly concerned with the question as to where she was to practice, and on what piano. The first thing next morning she reported the matter to Mr. Winscombe. That gentleman arrived later, with a lawyer. Selma was closely cross-examined. She gave her version of the case, only omitting the fact of Paul's disappearance.

Later in the day Mr. Winscombe had an interview with Sir Robert Ashington, the music patron and owner of the piano. He was a thin, scholarly-looking old gentleman with snow-white hair.

"Well, well!" he said, on hearing the clergyman's report. "What are we to do about it?"

"We have already notified the police, and Channing suggests that we might advertise it. If the people who bought the piano are a bona fide firm, they might be willing to come forward; but if, as is most likely, they got it for a song, they may keep quiet. It is easy enough to sell a Bechstein grand piano, and comparatively easy to alter the number, or to change it in such a manner that after a time they could dispose of it with safety."

"Do you suspect the family?"

The clergyman shrugged his shoulders.

"They are a terrible crowd, sir —terrible. They are certainly capable, either individually or collectively, of doing such a thing. The father, of course, is the most likely. He is in the piano trade, and would know how to go to work."

"What about the child?"

Mr. Winscombe smiled.

"She is splendid. She came to me this morning, and there were tears in her eyes. 'Oh, Mr. Winscombe,' she said, 'don't tell me this is the end! I shall go mad if I cannot go on playing!'"

There was a certain humidity about the eyes of the older man.

"Poor child!" he said. "Well, well, let us fix her up first. She had better have a room in some respectable house, and I dare say we can find her another piano. I saw Soltz two days ago. He says she is making astonishing strides."

Mr. Winscombe got busy. He had no room available in his own house, but he made arrangements with an American widow who lived with her son and daughter in a large house in Regent's Park. Her name was Mrs. Bouverie Bonnington. She was a warm-hearted, sympathetic woman, interested in social questions, clever, and well read. She had a music room and a grand piano which was seldom used in the daytime. Her son was at college, and her daughter was not musical. She gave Lena permission to go there and play whenever she liked.

An advertisement was put in the newspapers, but no reply was received, nor were the police ever able to solve the mystery of the vanished baby grand.

After a week or two Selma breathed more freely, but she was still frightened and entirely discontented with her lot. She suffered from sleeplessness. She had nightmares in which giants in green baize aprons played pitch and toss with enormous grand pianos that were forever about to drop on her head. She determined to marry her flashy young shop assistant at the earliest possible moment.

She told him that she had saved thirty five pounds out of her housekeeping money. Inspired by the thoughts of this noble endowment, he immediately conceived a great scheme by which it could be trebled by a cunning system of backing outsiders for small sums. Selma had no great faith in this, but after considerable discussion she advanced him ten pounds to experiment with.

Unfortunately for Selma's future life, the investment was surprisingly successful. It happened during the ensuing month that several most unlikely outsiders romped home to a place, and the ten pounds increased to forty-seven. The two capitalists got married, and went to live in rooms at Holloway. Selma's half share of the piano bought her married life.

## V

Selma's departure was the beginning of the disintegration of the whole Gabril family. Mischa went out to Canada, and they did not hear from him again. Katie wanted to come home and take Selma's place, but Mr. Gabril could not see that there was any point in his second daughter's suggestion. She was making good money; let her stop where she was. The rooms could look after themselves.

The three of them pigged along as best they could. Lena, absorbed in her work, would sometimes do a little sketchy dusting and cleaning, or shift the general disorder from one place to another. Katie would cook a scrappy meal. Mr. Gabril would come in, kick off his boots, and drink gin and water till he became maudlin.

A whole year went by—a year and eight months, and then Katie was suddenly taken ill. She had to go to a hospital and have an operation. It was not a serious operation, but in her anaemic and enfeebled condition it proved too much for her. She died under the anaesthetic.

Mr. Gabril was now rapidly running to seed. The firm still employed him, but he was intrusted with fewer and fewer orders. His income became automatically less. He began to regard Lena restlessly. It was quite time that she was making money. All this talk about a great career! He had been gambling on it, perhaps foolishly. She might be earning a pound a week or so at some honest job.

He went to see Mr. Winscombe, and explained his dissatisfaction.

"My dear sir," said that gentleman, u your daughter is getting on splendidly. Every one is delighted with her. They say she will be a great artist; but she must have time. It would be cruel to take her away now"

"How much time?"

"At least another two years. She might give lessons before then."

Two years! And Gabril had to keep her all that time? Oh, no, the game wasn't worth it! He growled an incoherent disapproval, borrowed five shillings from the clergyman, and came away. Something would have to be done.

That evening he took Lena severely to task.

"Now look here," he said. "That parson said you could give lessons. You'd better get busy and find some pupils. If you don't get pupils within the next week, I shall take you away and put you in a job."

It happened that evening that Selma called with her husband. She was querulous and tearful. The betting system had been a complete failure since their marriage, and she was going to have a baby. What were they going to do? Things were bad enough as it was. How could they afford a child as well, when George was in debt up to his eyes?

George did not give the impression of being in debt. He was well clothed and groomed, and his silver cigarette case was always flashing. He laughed indulgently at his wife. All would be well when the flat racing season started. He had had some very sound information straight out of the horse's nose bag.

"When are you going to start making all this money?" Selma suddenly asked Lena.

"What money, Selma?"

Even Mr. Gabril was aghast at this flippant reply. Money! What did the girl think she was doing all this ivory thumping for? For fun? For pleasure?

As a matter of fact, Lena had given the subject little thought. She had sometimes dreamed that she might one day be rich, and then she would like to go about helping people, even her own people, even Selma; but she did not associate the surging calls of her muse with making money. It was so much bigger and so far beyond that, so much more tremendous.

Of course, she wanted to do her duty. She didn't want to be mean, but she knew that in this social struggle to which she was born she had to fight her own battles.

"Perhaps I can get some pupils," she said defensively.

During the next few days she did look around and make inquiries; but pupils were not at all easy to secure. No one had heard of Lena Gabril. She looked too young to have the authority of a teacher.

She consulted Mr. Winscombe, and in the end, on his recommendation, a lady in the Camden Road engaged her to teach her two little girls. She was to be paid thirty shillings a term for giving the little girls twelve lessons each.

She broke the news to her father with triumph, but to her chagrin he received it angrily.

"Thirty shillings!" he whined. "What's the good of thirty shillings? You ought to be earning thirty pounds a term!"

Thirty pounds! Oh, dear! That would mean teaching forty little girls twelve hours each a term —four hundred and eighty hours in the term. When was she to get time for practice?

She would have to be cunning with her father, to humor him, to pretend that she was trying to get more and more pupils. The terrible menace of a "job" hung over her. She imagined herself in a pickle factory or a draper's shop, or perhaps out at service.

This drove her to work harder and harder at her piano. She said nothing about the kindness that Mrs. Bonnington was showing her. She pretended that she just went to a house, practiced in a room, and came away without seeing any one. She dreaded lest her father might call the house in Regent's Park, make a scene, borrow money, and behave in some disgraceful fashion. Some profound instinct of self-preservation prompted her to remain mute concerning the delightful lunches and teas and talks she had with Mrs. Bonnington and that lady's son and daughter. She had discovered a new world—a world which she had only been able dimly to imagine through the medium of music. She was emerging through the dark mists of her upbringing into a realm of light and understanding. She did not mean to let her father and stepsister drag her back without a bitter struggle.

## VI

Two months passed before the climax was reached. Lena had not been able to get any more pupils. Her father grew more and more vindictive, bitter, and inclined to violence. Mr. Gabril had been on one of his periodic orgies. One evening he arrived home, his eyes bloodshot and his breath whisky-laden. He had spent all his money, and he wanted more. Lena, of course, had none.

"Go and get some!" he roared.

"Where can I get any money?" she asked.

"You lazy little slut!" he screamed in a higher pitch. "Thirty shillings a term you earn, do you? I've been keeping you for seventeen years. To-morrow you'll come along with me. I'll get you a job with a pal of mine who runs a public house—that's what I'll do. He said he'd give you a job—barmaid, see? —in Kentish Town. You'll like it. A nice, merry life, plenty of boys and booze, see? Now, you go right along to that woman in the Camden Road, collect the thirty bob she owes you, and bring it back to me at once. Go on! Hurry up!"

"I couldn't do that," said Lena, coloring up. "I couldn't call there in the evening like this and ask for money."

"Oh, you couldn't, couldn't you?" said Mr. Gabril. "You couldn't do what your father tells you, couldn't you? Take that!"

He struck at her. Lena was expecting this. She put up her arm and parried the blow. She cowered against the wall. Her eyes narrowed.

"All right," she said quietly. "I'll go."

She put on her hat and cloak, tidied her hair before the broken mirror, and went slowly out.

After she had gone, Mr. Gabril felt ill. His heart was behaving queerly. He flopped upon the sofa and lay down.

"I want a drink," he kept on repeating. "That's what's the matter with me. Hope she'll be quick. I want a drink!"

He waited some time till a drowsiness crept over him, and then he sank into a drunken sleep. His next feeling was one of cold, discomfort, and wretchedness. He struggled through a coma to find himself. When consciousness came, it seemed only partial.

Where was he? What had happened? It was raw daylight, and he was lying on the sofa in the parlor. Why, yes, of course, he had had a bit of a binge; but why was he here? Where was Lena?

Lena! Why, yes, something had happened. Bit of a row, eh? He remembered now that he had sent her out to get some money. Where was she?

"Lena!" he called.

There was no answer. He got up and stumbled to the girl's bedroom. She was not there. Where the devil was she? He visited each room in turn, and wandered out to the staircase.

It was broad daylight, it must be nearly midday, and she had gone out last night. What had happened to her? An accident? Perhaps she had jumped into the canal because he struck her. Girls were like that— silly, hysterical creatures; but Lena wasn't exactly the sort.

What was he to do? He felt ill, and he had no money. He crawled back to the sofa.

He lay there for hours in a kind of torpor, hoping that Lena would return. There was a little food in the house, but he felt too ill to eat anything. Once he worked himself up into a violent fit of rage. He swore and blasphemed loudly; but, finding that this only made him feel worse, he finally desisted.

When the room began to get dark again, he became desperate. He scribbled a note to Selma, telling her to come and see him at once. He got a boy on the floor below to take it, on a promise of sixpence. Then he waited in the increasing gloom.

It was three hours before Selma came. She came alone. He cursed her for being so long, and she lost her temper. When she heard of Lena's disappearance, her expression became blacker still. When her father suggested accident or suicide, she cried out savagely:

"Not she, you fool! That's not her luck. 1 felt it from the first. She's gone to her rich friends!"

"Where do they live?"

"I don't know—somewhere in Regent's Park. I've never been there. I don't know their name."

"I'll make the devils pay for this! How can we find them?"

"Mr. Winscombe would know."

"That's right, curse him! You go and find out from him. Got any money, Selma? If so, for God's sake go and get me a drink first!"

"I haven't any money for drinks for you, but I'll go round to Mr. Winscombe."

Mr. Gabril growled, and Selma went out of the house. She felt tired herself, but there was a sense of grim satisfaction in being able to hand her stepsister over to her father's vengeance.

Mr. Winscombe was out, but he was expected in. He kept Selma waiting half an hour. When he arrived, he said that he knew nothing about Lena's disappearance. He had not seen Mrs. Bonnington for weeks. However, he reluctantly gave Selma the American, lady's name and address.

Armed with this weapon of vengeance, Selma returned to her father. She found him lying face downward by the fireplace. He was dead.

She gave a feeble scream when she felt his stiff body. Then she stood up and looked around her. The instinct of self-preservation was fortified by her condition. She had no love for her father. She looked at the sticks of furniture, and reflected. She knew her father had no money; but there were three rooms furnished in a way. The whole lot would fetch several pounds. There was an unborn child to consider, and the flat racing season was not proving profitable to George. Who should have this furniture, if not she?

She looked at the crumpled paper in her hand—Lena's address. What should she do about that? If Lena had gone to live with these people, she couldn't prevent her. She was a little frightened of educated people, and, indeed, a little frightened of Lena herself. Besides, if the girl returned, she might claim her share of the furniture.

Selma flung the paper in the fireplace. Let Lena go her own way. Let her rot!

VII

One spring afternoon, seven years later, Selma was walking down Great Portland Street. Under her arm she was carrying a bundle of washing. She and her husband and three children now lived in a slum off the Euston Road. She was taking the washing back to a woman she worked for in Oxford Street.

Taking the narrow turning that runs at the back of the Queen's Hall, her eye alighted on a portrait that struck her as being familiar. Underneath it was a name in large black type—"Lena Gabrielski." Then, in red type, were the words:

First appearance since her brilliantly successful American tour.

Selma had hardly recovered from her astonishment at recognizing Lena's portrait when a woman came hurriedly out through the artists' door. It was Lena herself. The two women looked straight into each other's eyes. Lena was the first to speak.

"Selma!" she gasped.

Selma was entirely non-plused. She did not know how to act. She shifted the bundle of washing self-consciously from one arm to the other.

"Why do you call yourself that funny long name?" she said at random.

Lena glanced at the poster.

"Oh, that was my agent's idea. How are you, Selma?"

Selma sniffed.

"All right," she said.

She was consumed with the consciousness of jarring contrast. Her own slatternliness, her bundle, and this other woman with the clothes, the manner, the faint perfume of the well-bred! Could it be possible that they had the same father?

Selma had never really known Lena, even when they lived together; and now they were farther separated by seven long years of alien, unknown experiences. Selma felt shy and ashamed. She turned to walk away. Lena hurried after her.

"Selma! Selma, what is it? I tried to find you once or twice, but you had moved, and no one knew your address."

Selma didn't know what prompted her to do it, but she felt a sudden desire to hurt Lena, and to hurt herself even more. She stopped and said bitterly:

"Do you know it was me and Paul that stole your piano? We sold it and shared the money."

Lena gave a little gasp. It was her turn to cry, but a smile struggled through her tears. She pressed her stepsister's arm.

"Never mind, Selma! You did me a great service. If you had not taken it, I should never perhaps have met my—my husband. And we're so happy, Selma!"

"You—married!"

"Yes—I married Mrs. Bonnington's son. We live at Hampstead. Won't you come and see us? I'd like to help you, Selma."

For a moment the elder woman wavered. She dug her hard fingers tighter into the bundle of washing before she spoke. Then she said savagely:

"No, I don't want your charity. We're like—like different animals—that's what it is. What's the good of my coming to see you? You go your way, and I'll go mine!"

And, gripping her bundle, she hurried away.


London Discovers "Uncle Abe"

London has taken over the spirit of Abraham Lincoln and now shares its influence with the United States. Historians, poets, and dramatists write of the great American. All London, and soon all England, will be happier and wiser in knowing about "The great heart of humanity."

An event is happening in London which every American ought to know of. It may not in itself appear to be of great importance, but on reflection it becomes a matter of pregnant significance. In an obscure suburb, buried away among shops and booths, is a small theater with the somewhat grandiloquent title of the Lyric Opera House. A year or so ago not one Londoner in ten thousand could have told you where the Lyric Opera House was. Then one day some enthusiasts from Birmingham, with a passion for reforming the stage, came to London. Finding themselves crowded out of all the West End theaters, where revues and pajama farces were in complete sway, they came across this obscure theater and put on a play. It was a purely experimental play, [the kind of thing that any theatrical expert would have prophesied as being good for a few matinees, or probably a week's run at a loss. The play concerned the life of an American. It is true, it was a great—probably the greatest American who ever lived. But that was all it was. It could not be called a good play in any sense. It certainly had none of the ingredients of a popular success. There was no plot, no sensational development, very little humor, and, strangest of all, no love interest. It just portrayed the character, and some of the human episodes in the political career, of a rugged man.

But the Londoner, who is slow in the uptake, but persistent when he wants a thing, gradually began to trace his footsteps, as though compelled by some mesmeric force, in the direction of the Lyric Opera House. To say that the play caught on would be too mild a way of expressing the peculiar grip which the life of Abraham Lincoln has got upon us. London has fallen under the spell of "Uncle Abe." The thing has been an enormous popular success. It has been going on months, and still every performance is crowded out. Only last week a bishop drove up. He had come to town specially from the country to see the play, and he could not get a seat! Now everybody knows the Lyric Opera House and is anxious to direct you thither. But it is n't only the box-office which interests us. The play has been more than a popular success. It has been a symbol, an inspiration.

The people who crowd the theater are not a clique of literary or theatrical dilettante; they are the people. You see them sitting there in rows,—the seats are all low-priced,—mixed up and familiar, princes and publicans, bankers, bishops (I hope he got a seat the next night), clerks and green-grocers, horsy-looking men and poets, little shop girls and old duchesses. They are peculiarly silent, thrilled, moved. If you ask them, they can't tell you why, but they say, "It's wonderful," and they go away and come again and again.

How much of this wonder may be due to the genius of Mr. John Drinkwater, who wrote the play and produced it, or to the clever company who interpret it, is difficult to determine. I have spoken to hundreds of people who have been, and many have criticized the acting or the producing or the play itself; but I have not met one who did not think that somehow it was "wonderful" and they wanted to go again. The solution may be that in the mind of Abraham Lincoln we find a salve, healing the complicated disruption of our own present troubles. The conditions are somewhat analogous. We observe the reactions of our own distresses through this spectacle of great simplicity. It is as though we had been groping in the dark for something which we had lost, when a friend appears who produces an electric torch, and we observe that that which we had lost is lying at our feet. We recall the phenomena of our own upheaval, the basic causes of war and civil strife. The greed and intolerance of those in high places, the insincerity and chop-logic of politicians, the sycophantic attitude of place-seekers, the machinations of profiteers, the fear and cowardice and heroism of the individual man, and through it all this one simple man, of inflexible purpose, high courage, broad vision, and unbounded humanity. His horror and loathing of war permeate the play. He is incapable of bitterness and hatred. He can hate only an idea. He represents to us what is best in us, the attitude we ourselves would like to take in our best moments. When the dear old society lady rejoices in the slaughter of many thousands of "these disgusting rebels,"—we can almost hear her say "disgusting Huns,"—the heart of Lincoln is as nearly stirred to hate as it is capable of. He turns on her in a flood of scorn and orders her from the house. That was not the spirit in which he plunged his country into war. Men were dying that a broader humanity might emerge. The colored man should be free, the brother of the white man, not the slave. All men were equal in the sight of God, and all men must obey the dictates of this human impulse. Let justice be done though the heavens fall, but justice with mercy, and with your eye always fixed upon the ultimate goal.

It was an American who toasted "Our country. In her intercourse with foreign nations may she always be in the right; but our country, right or wrong."

But Lincoln was bigger than that. And it is because we believe that he was bigger than that that we rejoice in him. We do not believe that he would have backed his country in what he believed to be an unjust war. He would have been a rebel. He would rather have died at the stake. One sees in him the birth of a force acting socially rather than nationally. That is why in these days when national issues are involved and confused, when they who, we are told by our governments, are one day our friends and another day our enemies, we turn to Lincoln as we would turn to a draft of water at a surfeited banquet in an overheated room. And there dawns upon us at the Lyric Opera House a new and comforting generalization. It is this: there could never be serious trouble between England and America, because the day is dawning when things are acting socially rather than nationally. The workers of the world are becoming as great a force as governments themselves, indeed greater. It will no longer be possible to wave a flag, put head-lines in the newspapers, and send a band into the street and say, "We are at war!" Government is going to be by the people and for the people. There might conceivably be some quite serious point of dispute between the governments, but the people will require to know all about it. And then there will be a national cleavage. Parties will be formed on each side favoring the other country's point of view. There will be no national unity in the old sense. The world—or in any case, for the time being, our world—will act socially.

That which is called "industrial unrest" is not a purely material thing. It does not concern only work and wages. It is a spiritual revolt. Five million men were slain on the battle-fields of Europe, and nine tenths of those men were sent to their deaths without being consulted or without fully understanding the fundamental cause of the strife. And this holocaust has made the people of these various countries suspicious. They are for the most part patient, longsuffering people, good sportsmen, quite willing to die in a good cause; but they are beginning to feel that if this sort of thing is going to happen often, they would like to know all about it. Indeed, they would like to be consulted. Incidentally, they want to make it impossible to happen again.

The London cockney made as good showing in the war as any, and he was in it from the very first. He is not very clever perhaps, but he's no fool. He doesn't believe all the newspapers tell him. The war has broadened his outlook considerably. He has rubbed shoulders with every other national, white and colored, in all parts of the world. Whereas before he may not have traveled farther than from Putney to the Welsh Harp, or from Hendon to Brighton, now he is familiar with France and Italy, Greece, Egypt, Mesopotamia, and India. He has boxed with Australians, made love to French girls, and swapped cigarettes with German prisoners. Death has been his near and familiar companion for four and a half years. And on the top of it all he is thoroughly surfeited with cant. These newspapers and old ladies and arm-chair patriots, phew! Suddenly he finds himself listening to some one he understands, a big and simple citizen like himself, albeit a foreigner. A fine old boy, "Uncle Abe." No nonsense about him. He doesn't get tied up in a knot with highfalutin rhetoric. He hasn't got one eye on the enemy and the other on the next general election. He doesn't say one thing and mean another. He's big, universal, and his spirit is communicable.

This is what the cockney thinks, the cockney who has seen the world and carried other men's burdens upon his back. And his spirit, too, is communicable. That is why the dowager duchesses go, too, and the war exploiters and the old clubmen and the arm-chair patriots. They go and feel humbled, universal, as though their spirit were being transposed from the minor key of their small self-centered lives into a broader key of a great composition. They cannot remain unmoved, and so, while they cannot explain it, they say it's "wonderful."

Yes, London has fallen to "Uncle Abe." The curtain has come down on the great drama, and our voices are hushed. We know that it is too soon for its significance to come home to us. We are still dazed and bewildered. The eager faces of the young men who will never return are still with us. The sound of their laughter is still fresh in our ears. In such a condition men cannot think or forget or even remember. It will take a hundred years. And so they dance and dance and dance, as though they were trying to readjust the normal rhythm of human intercourse, so long a broken discord. And when everything seems meaningless, what better occupation can there be than dancing? In time the systole and the diastole will resume its healthy beat. Beneath the hatred and malice and misunderstanding we are learning to know that, as Nurse C a veil discovered, "Patriotism is not enough." Beneath it all there remains the great heart of humanity, the great heart of Lincoln, beating for our eternal good. London is wiser and better and vastly happier for her discovery of "Uncle Abe."


Stacy Aumonier – A Short Biography

Stacy Aumonier was born at Hampstead Road near Regent's Park, London on 31st March 1877.

He came from a family with a strong and sustained tradition in the visual arts; sculptors and painters.

In 1890 the teenage Aumonier attended Cranleigh School in Surrey. Although he would later write critically about English public schools (with articles for the London Evening Standard and New York Times) in how they tried to impose conformity on students, records indicate that he integrated well into Cranleigh. Aumonier was a passionate cricket player, belonged to the Literary and Debating Society, and, in his final year, became a prefect.

On leaving school it seemed the family tradition of the visual arts would be his career path. In particular his early talents were that of a landscape painter. He exhibited paintings at the Royal Academy in 1902 and 1903, and 1908. An exhibition of his work would later be held at the Goupil Gallery in London in 1911.

In 1907 he married the international concert pianist, Gertrude Peppercorn, at West Horsley in Surrey. She herself was the daughter of a landscape painter (Arthur Douglas Peppercorn, occasionally cited as 'the English Corot'.) A son, Timothy, was born in 1921.

A year after his marriage, Aumonier began a brief career in a second branch of the arts at which he enjoyed outstanding success—as a stage performer writing and performing his own sketches.

The Observer newspaper commented that "...the stage lost in him a real and rare genius, he could walk out alone before any audience, from the simplest to the most sophisticated, and make it laugh or cry at will."

In 1915, Aumonier published a short story 'The Friends' which was well received (and voted one of the best short stories of 1915 by the Boston Magazine, Transcript).

Despite his age being 40 in 1917 he was called up for service in World War I. He began as a private in the Army Pay Corps, and then transferred as a draughtsman in the Ministry of National Service.

By now he had four books published—two novels and two books of short stories—and his occupation is recorded with the Army Medical Board as 'author.'

In the mid-1920s, Aumonier received the shattering diagnosis that he had contracted tuberculosis. In the last few years of his life, he would spend long spells in various sanatoria, some better than others. In a letter to his friend, Rebecca West, written shortly before his death, he described the debilitating conditions in a sanatorium in Norfolk during the winter of 1927, where the dampness was so severe that a newspaper left beside the bed would feel "sodden to the touch in the morning."

Shortly before his death, Stacy Aumonier sought treatment in Switzerland, but died of the disease in Clinique La Prairie at Clarens beside Lake Geneva on 21st December 1928. He was 55.

Whilst Aumonier's works are now slowly coming back into circulation at the time of his death his works were extremely popular and his loss was a profound tragedy for literary society.

The chief fiction critic of The Observer, Gerald Gould wrote: "His gifts were almost fantastically various; they embraced all the arts; but it was the charm and generosity of his personality which made him—what he unquestionably was—one of the most popular men of his generation." It went on: "The things he wrote will be remembered when the company of his friends (no man had more friends, or more devoted and admiring) are with him in the grave; but just now, to those who knew him, the thing most vividly present is the charm and wisdom of the man they knew."

Of his general appearance and manner Gerald Cumberland gives us this interesting set of observations: "A distinguished man, this—distinguished both in mind and appearance. Self-conscious. Perhaps. Why not? His hair is worn a trifle long, and it is arranged so that his fine forehead, broad and high, may be fully revealed. Round his neck is a very high collar and a modern stock. When in repose, his face has a look of shy eagerness; his quick eyes glance here and there gathering a thousand impressions to be stored up in his brain. It is the face of a man extremely sensitive to external stimulus; one feels that his brain works not only rapidly, but with great accuracy. And at heart, he takes himself and his work seriously, though he likes on occasion to pretend that he is only a philanderer."

In literary terms Aumonier was amongst the best short story writers these shores have produced.

The Nobel Prize winning author John Galsworthy called him "A real master of the short story. The first essential in a short-story writer is the power of interesting sentence by sentence. Aumonier had this power in prime degree. You do not have to 'get into' his stories. He is especially notable for investing his figures with the breadth of life within a few sentences." Galsworthy asserted that Aumonier "is never heavy, never boring, never really trivial; interested himself, he keeps us interested. At the back of his tales, there is belief in life and a philosophy of life, and of how many short story writers can that be said? ...He follows no fashion and no school. He is always himself. And can't he write? Ah! Far better than far more pretentious writers. Nothing escapes his eye, but he describes without affectation or redundancy, and you sense in him a feeling for beauty that is never obtruded. He gets values right, and that is to say nearly everything. The easeful fidelity of his style has militated against his reputation in these somewhat posturing times. But his shade may rest in peace, for in this volume, at least he will outlive nearly all the writers of his day." In summing his up Galsworthy suggested that, through his stories, he would "outlive all the writers of his day."

James Hilton (author of Goodbye, Mr Chips and Lost Horizon) said "I think his very best works ought to be included in any anthology of the best short stories ever written." He cited 'The Octave of Jealously' as his favourite short story for the March 1939 edition of Good Housekeeping saying it was a "bitterly brilliant tale."

Rebecca West said of his writing in 1922 that his ability to blend reality with the imaginary was "the envy of all artists."

## Stacy Aumonier – A Concise Bibliography

More than 87 short stories in more than 25 magazines, and in 6 volumes published during Aumonier's lifetime.

Among more than 20 other magazines, his work appeared in Argosy Magazine, John O' London's Weekly, The Strand Magazine and The Saturday Evening Post, as well as being anthologized, and adapted for film and television.

### Short Story Collections

The Golden Windmill & Other Stories (1921)
The Friends & Other Stories (1917)
Miss Bracegirdle & Other Stories (1923)

### Novels

Olga Bardel (1916)
Three Bars Interval (1917)
Just Outside (1917)
The Querrils (1919)
One After Another (1920)
Heartbeat (1922)

### Other Works

A volume of 14 Character Studies: Odd Fish (1923)

A volume of 15 Essays: Essays of Today and Yesterday (1926)

www.ingramcontent.com/pod-product-compliance
Lightning Source LLC
Chambersburg PA
CBHW061453170626
46811CB00004B/1493